CLOSE SHAVES

Classic Stories on the Edge

CLOSE SHAVES

Classic Stories on the Edge

Edited by John Long

ICS BOOKS, Inc.
Merrillville, Indiana

CLOSE SHAVES *Classic Stories on the Edge*
Copyright © 1997 edited by John Long

Published by:
ICS BOOKS, Inc.
1370 E. 86th Place
Merrillville, IN 46410
800-541-7323

Library of Congress Cataloging-in-Publication Data
Close shaves : stories on the edge / edited by John Long.
    p. cm.
  ISBN 0-57034-032-3
  1. Adventure and adventurers. 2. Wilderness survival. 3. Near
-death experiences. I. Long, John, 1953-
G525.C588 1996   96-1297
904--dc20   CIP

TABLE OF CONTENTS

INTRODUCTION: CLOSE SHAVES

It might have started with Stevenson's *Kidnapped*, or London's South Pacific stories. Or perhaps all those Hardy Boy Adventures I devoured during required study hall at the Southern California Military Academy, where I was shipped off for seventh grade. Whatever the source, early on I became hooked on adventure stories. The addiction grew when I started running rivers and rock climbing. Though fictional accounts were high in romance, they never felt to have the same gravity as authentic accounts about authentic people; and this later genre—the true life close shave—became my favorite. Some fifteen years ago I started photocopying some of the true shaves that I never wanted to lose. This volume is a sampling of those stories, with the emphasis on outdoor/action adventure. All the usual themes—animal attacks, climbing epics, astounding airplane tales, or survival yarns of any ilk—have provided grist for thousands of books. Rather than specialize on one theme, however, I've patched together a collection of various kinds of stories for the sake of variety. No matter how riveting the stories are individually, too much of the same jades me in the end, whereas a medley keeps my interest sharp. I trust others will feel the same way.

These stories are more than mere page turners. They are events in which the kaleidoscope of people's lives was wrenched ninety degrees. The light shifted, and suddenly the colors and shards of glass settled into chaotic arrangements. The landscape grew threatening, desperate, even hopeless. But they carried on for many reasons, reason clouded by attempts to define and analyze, but brought into sharp focus when we experience the shave through the written word. The search for meaning is always the business of the individual, but if these stories suggest nothing else, they suggest that adventure and life are the same thing; that to deny one is to limit the prospects of the other; that all adventures invariably point toward the mystery of being alive. For those who fought through the Long Night to the light of day, their stories are a timeless reminder of this.

RISK AND RECREATION

by Edward E. Leslie

NOVEMBER 13, 1942

On the second day of the four-day Battle of Guadalcanal, the cruiser JUNEAU is sunk, resulting in a loss of 560 men. Another 140 sailors climb into life rafts or congregate in the water around them.

Seaman Allen Clifton Heyn, gunner's mate, second class, had been about to relieve another sailor on the I.I. stern gun. The man was still wearing the phone set, and Heyn saw his mouth drop open. An instant later a torpedo struck at midship. The explosion slammed Heyn against a gun mount and knocked him out cold. When he came to, oil was falling in such a quantity that he thought it was rain.

Heyn later recalled the scene for a debriefing officer:

"There was smoke and there was fellows laying all around there and parts of their gunshields torn apart and the fantail where I was sticking almost straight up in the air. It was so slippery that you couldn't walk up it and guys that was still able to climb over the side couldn't walk up. They were crawling over the side and holding on the lifeline trying to pull themselves further aft and jump over. And they were jumping over and bumping into each other.

It was still so smoky and all, you couldn't quite see and I see still hazy and I knew I had to get up and get off of there. I was afraid the suction would pull me down. When I went to get up, I felt this pain in my foot and I couldn't get my foot across the instep of it and I couldn't get loose. It was only a few seconds, and the water was closing in around the ship and there was just this little bit of it left. And I knew that I had to get off but couldn't and there was a lot of kapok life jackets laying around deck.

I grabbed one of them in my arms and held it. I didn't even put it on. The water closed in around the ship, and we went down. And I gave up, I just thought that there wasn't a chance at all, everything just run through my head. And you could see all [the] objects in the water, all the fellows and everything and after we were under the surface I don't know how far but the sheet of iron or whatever it was, it was released and my foot came loose and then the buoyancy from the life jacket brought me back to the surface."

The oil was two inches thick on the sea, and all around Heyn swirled blueprints, drawings of the Juneau, and many rolls of toilet paper. He was groggy and unable to see anyone else around him. He wondered dully if he was the only one who had made it. He put on the life jacket and began paddling around.

A doughnut life raft popped up out of the ocean in front of him. He had just gotten a grip on it when he heard a man cry for help. It was a boatswain's mate, second class, who had worked in the Juneau's post office. His leg had been blown off and he could not swim. Heyn pushed the doughnut over to him and helped him into it.

Other survivors soon made their way to the raft and climbed or were pulled in. "Everybody was kind of scared at first," Heyn remembered. "Some of them couldn't swim, they were afraid they'd lose their grip and drown."

A number of B-17 Flying Fortresses flew low over the water, and the pilots waved to the men, giving them the hope—a false one, as it turned out—that they would soon be picked up. The Juneau, which had sustained crippling damage before being hit by the torpedo that sank her, had been part of a makeshift convoy of five ships, all of which had been put out of commission and had withdrawn from the battle. The survivors in the doughnut thought they might be picked up by one of the other vessels. The ranking officer of the convoy, however, had decided that with a submarine in the area, a rescue operation was too risky, and he gave orders that the ships were to keep sailing. The Juneau's men saw the masts disappear over the horizon.

Late in the afternoon it rained heavily. Although the visibility was poor, every few minutes one man or another would call out that he could see a vessel, but all the reports were false. When the rain stopped, Heyn's raft was joined by two others. Each of them was a circular float with netting over the doughnut hole. They were designed to hold large numbers of men, but these three were badly overcrowded with survivors, most of whom were at least partially immersed in the water.

"I should say there was about 140 of us when we all got together. Some of them were in very bad shape. Their arms and legs were torn off. And one of them, I could see his skull. You could see the red part inside where his head had been split open, torn open in places. They were all crying together and very down and wondering if anybody was ever going to pick them up. And they thought, well, at least tomorrow there will be somebody out here.

That night was very hard because most of the fellows who were wounded badly were crying and, you know, groaning about their pains and everything. They were all in agony. And in the morning this fellow that I said that had his head open, his hair had turned gray just like as if he was an old man. It had turned gray right over night.

Everybody had so much oil on them, their ears and eyes would burn and the salt water would hurt so much that you couldn't hardly look around to see if anybody was there. You couldn't recognize each other unless you knew each other very well before the ship went down, or unless it was somebody that you'd recognize by his voice. So all these rolls of tissue paper were floating around there. If you unrolled them, in the middle they were dry and we'd take that and wipe our eyes out with them and ease the pain a lot and wipe our faces off a little."

Lieutenant Blodgett, the Juneau's gunnery officer, took charge. He thought that land was nearby and was determined that they paddle to it. The sailors formed the doughnuts into a line and tied them together. The ablest men got into the first two, straddled the floats and paddled. They worked in shifts throughout that day and the night that followed, with Blodgett navigating by the stars. Yet they did not seem to make any progress. The rafts moved poorly in the sea.

On the third day, a Flying Fortress dropped a rubber lifeboat some distance from them. They could see it occasionally when it rose on the crests of high waves. They wanted to retrieve it because its design made it move better than the ones they were in; with it they might be able to make more progress. Some men were going to swim for it, but sharks were spotted in the water. In the end Heyn and some others detached one of the doughnuts and paddled over to it. They triggered its self-inflating mechanism, and one of them paddled it to the other rafts while the rest returned in the doughnut.

Most of the castaways agreed that the best use for the new boat would be to house the seriously wounded; at least they would be dry there. The several uninjured sailors who had already climbed into it, however, had other ideas.

"It was towards evening now, and there were three men in this rubber raft. They hollered back to us that they had decided to go for land, that it would be better that they go for land and send us help. But all these fellows that was on the doughnuts who were very sick and wounded didn't want that. They wanted to be put in the rubber raft and all stay together. They felt, well, it was much easier there than it was on the doughnut. And why should those three go in that rubber raft and leave us here? It looked like we would be goners that way. Everybody figured that anyway.

Well, they said they were going anyway, so they unsecured the line and paddled off. And all these fellows that was hurt bad was hollering for them to come back but they kept going."

A few of those left behind were even more desperate to reach shore. Wooden planks floated around the doughnuts; the men held on to these and swam away. One of them realized after a time that he would not make it, and so he returned to the rafts, but Heyn never saw any of the others again; presumably they drowned or were devoured by sharks.

Heyn estimated that there were now only fifty of the Juneau's men left alive. Some of them did not have shirts and were suffering terribly from sunburn. Those, like Heyn, who still had their clothes fared much better, he thought, because the oil had soaked into the cloth and afforded them an extra measure of protection.

On the fourth day the sea turned rough, and the rafts became detached from one another. The twelve men in Heyn's doughnut tried to keep it close to the other, but the waves drove them away.

Before long the deprivations began to affect them mentally. When aircraft would fly over, a few of the more rational men would wave at them and try to get the attention of their crews. The seamen who had become disoriented, however, would castigate the signalers, telling them to ignore the planes because the military did not want to save them and meant to leave them on the ocean to die. Heyn was not one of those to despair, being certain that only the continued fighting was preventing the dispatching of a vessel to pick them up.

"They knew we were there, I knew that, so when they could send a ship they'd come. Some of the guys was kinda disappointed and pretty low so they sorta gave up. There's one fellow, he was a gunner's mate from the Juneau, second class. Well, he kept swallowing salt water all the time and he'd let his head fall down in the water and swallow it and he'd begin to get very dopey and dreary. He couldn't help himself at all so I held him up. I held him that way all afternoon. Toward night he got stiff and I told the other fellows.

I said, 'Well, how about holding him a while? I can't hold him, I've got all to do to hold myself.' And they said they wouldn't do it, they were arguing and fighting among themselves a lot. And I said, 'I felt his heart and his wrists and I couldn't feel any beating.' I figured he was dead and I said to them, 'Well, I'm going to let him go.'

And George Sullivan, the oldest brother of the Sullivans, he said to me, 'You can't do that.' He said, 'It's against all regulations of the Navy. You can't bury a man at sea without having official orders from some captain or the Navy Department or something like that.' And I knew he was delirious and there was something wrong with him and all, but they wouldn't let me let him go.

I said to them, 'Well, you hold him,' and they wouldn't hold him. So it went on that way for a little while. His legs were hanging down in the water a little way below mine when a shark bit his leg right below the knee. He didn't move or say anything. That was enough for me. I figured, well I'm going to drop him. There isn't any sense holding a dead man. So we took his dog tag off, this one fellow did, and said a prayer for him and let him float away.

At night it was so cold for the fellows who didn't have no clothes, we'd try to huddle them among us to keep them warm under the water. The sharks kept getting worse in the daytime, and you could see them around us all the time. We'd kick them with our feet and splash the water and they'd keep away. But at night you'd get drowsy and you'd kinda fall asleep and you wouldn't see them coming. As night went on they'd come and they'd grab a guy every once in a while and bite him. And once they did, they wouldn't eat him altogether, then they'd just take a piece of him and go away and drown him. He'd scream and holler and everything but there wasn't anything we could do to help."

The weather was causing the raft's canvas to tear, and the netting was wearing out. Afraid the doughnut would fall apart, the men busied themselves repairing it: "We were trying to secure it together all the time."

That night a man announced that he was going to swim for land. Heyn and the others repeatedly dragged him back into the raft, but eventually he got away from them. He had made only fifty yards when a shark grabbed him, "and that's the last we seen of him."

"And then the fellows got kind of ideas that the ship was sunk under us, sitting on the bottom. You could swim down there at night and get something to eat and all them kinda things, and I was beginning to believe them. They said they could see a light down there and this one fellow kept saying, 'If it's down there what are we staying up here for, let's go down there and get something to eat then.' So I said, 'You show me the way down there.' So he dives under water and I went after him and I never did find nothing down there, no hatch or anything like he said was there. And I got my sense again and I knew what I was doing and I didn't believe him anymore.

The fifth day was coming up. There were only two or three guys gone but things were getting even worse. The guys were fighting among themselves. If you bumped into one of them, he'd get mad and holler at you. And they did talk a lot about home and what they were going to do, and a lot of them said if they could get on an island, they'd stay there, they'd never go back to the Navy. They didn't want to see it no more. And they were mad that they were left out there in the water. It wasn't fair that they should be left like that! The ships went off and didn't pick them up."

The men without shirts were in agony. Heyn thought their skin looked as if it had been scraped with a razor. Some of them were saying that they would rather drown themselves than endure anymore. After dark, George Sullivan announced that he was going to take a bath. He stripped and went into the ocean, swimming a little way from the doughnut. Heyn thought that the whiteness of his body "flashed" and attracted the shark...The sharks took two other sailors that night as well.

On the morning of the sixth day, with the sea rough, a gull landed on the raft. The men grabbed for him, but he took off. He returned, however, and this time he was caught and his neck was wrung. There were only three or four men left to share the small carcass.

"We just floated in the water and talked together and the sharks kept bothering us all the time. We'd keep beating them off and try to keep away from them, and the planes flew over all the time again. But they didn't pay any attention to us.

Well, another night went on and the next day, this gunner's mate, his name was Stewart, he said that there was a hospital ship there and we were going to go over to it. There were three of us—him, me and another fellow—and he said that we should swim over to it and leave the doughnut. We didn't know whether to or not. You hated to leave it there because you knew if you got in the water, you were gone. So he dove in the water and swam off and he just kept swimming out over the water and he wouldn't turn around. You could see the sharks going after him and he swam and kicked and swam. And he hollered to us to come and get him with the raft, to paddle towards him but he kept swimming the other way. We paddled towards him and he finally got tired. He turned around and came towards us and he got back before the sharks got him.

But that night it got cold again. He had thrown all his clothes away and he didn't have a thing and he wanted me to give him my clothes. But I said no, there's no sense to that. And he said, 'Well, then I'm going down to the ship and get a clean suit. I got a lot of them in my locker.' He also said, 'I got a case of peaches in my gun mount.'"

Several times Heyn talked him out of swimming down to the Juneau, and to keep him warm he set Stewart between himself and the third man, a Mexican-American whose name Heyn did not know. Before long, however, Stewart decided that he had had enough of hardship and the cold. He went into the ocean and swam until the sharks took him.

Now there were only two of them left. They spent the day talking and securing the raft.

"We were at each end with our feet kinda up in the water so we could fight the sharks off better. That night we got sleepy and we dozed off, I guess, because a shark grabbed him and tore his leg off below, just jaggedy like. And he complained, he said to me that somebody was stabbing him with a knife. I said how can anybody stab you out here? There's nobody but the us two.

And he swore at me and called me all kinds of names and said I had to get him to a doctor. I guess I was delirious, because I was paddling and paddling in the water there. I didn't know where I was going, I was just paddling, trying to get him to a doctor. Well, finally he screamed and hollered and he came over to me and I held his arm and then I could see what it was. I knew that he had been bit by a shark and I held him and the shark came up and it just grabbed him underneath and kept eating him from the bottom and pulling on him. Well, I couldn't hold him anymore.

The sharks just pulled him down under the water and he gone. It seemed like the night would never end. I was the only one left.

The next day I floated around some more and it went on like that for the next couple days and in the morning of the last day, which was the ninth day, I began to get delirious. I see these guys come up out of the water. It looked like they had rifles on their backs and I'd holler to them and they said they were up there on guard duty. They'd come up from each hatch on the ship. Well, I asked them how it was. And they said the ship was all right, you could go down there and get something dry and eat. So I said to them, well, I'll come over there by you and go down with you. I swam over to them and they disappeared. I went back. I done that twice. Each time they disappeared when I got there. And then my head got clear and something told me to hang on a little longer."

At noon on November 22, 1942, a Catalina seaplane flew over the raft, circled, and then departed. Heyn was sure that, like the crews of all the other aircraft, this one would not bother to help him, that they would feel he was not worth the effort. "Or maybe they didn't know what I was because I was all black. I might have been a Jap for all they knew."

In the afternoon the plane came back, circled him again, and dropped smoke bombs around the doughnut. Heyn allowed himself to feel some measure of hope. The fliers were guiding a vessel to him, he decided, and he was exactly correct. In a little while he saw a mast on the horizon. It was the destroyer USS Ballard, which, when she got close, lowered a small boat and picked him up.

He was delirious and suffering from shock. He had severe headaches as a result of his having been slammed into the Juneau's gun mount, and his foot was broken. "I was sick all over," he told a navy interrogator in 1944, "and I don't know, I was sorta wore out."

Only ten of the *Juneau's* crew are known to have survived. Six of those were in other doughnuts and were rescued by another Catalina. The three men who had taken the rubber raft reached a small island, where they were cared for by friendly natives and a European merchant. They were taken off the island by a Catalina.

The five Sullivan brothers who had been on board the destroyer died either when the ship sank or on the sea afterward. They became posthumously famous, and a film was made of their lives. The navy honored them by naming a destroyer after them.

As for Heyn himself, he was initially taken to Espiritu Santo and then, after about two weeks, was transferred to the USS Solace. He was moved to an army hospital at Fiji, where he remained until his bed was needed for other patients, and then he was shifted to a navy dispensary.

He stayed on Fiji for nine months before he volunteered for submarine duty, making no secret of his desire to avenge the Juneau. On his first patrol, his boat was credited with sinking five ships and damaging four others. Heyn was a gunner, and some of the vessels were sunk by guns. "It made me feel awful good when we got them. One of them was a troop ship and it was full of them. You could see them hanging all over the sides and everything." No prisoners were taken aboard the submarine.

He was awaiting another assignment when he was debriefed by a Lieutenant Porter. Heyn said he wanted to continue in the submarine service. Porter asked where he would like to be stationed, and he replied, "It wouldn't make any difference as long as it's out in the Pacific somewhere."

IMPROBABLE MARKSMAN

by John Long

Since it had not rained in nearly two weeks, which defied every native's memory, the river had waned to a trickle, and we could hike the normally flooded streambed, skating over river stones submerged for a thousand years, stones that would never feel sunlight until the snarled green ceiling had receded and by then the stones would be silt, flushed into larger rivers, washed into deltas, into the ocean.

We were five people: a native Iban chief whose torso was a tattooed cavalcade of deer and snakes and arcane emblems, and whose bare feet crunched driftwood littering the pebbly route; two young Iban hunters who carried our provisions in swollen rattan packs and whose mouthfuls of betal nut yielded a shocking red spit that stained the river stones like the spore of a wounded boar; a twenty-two-year-old Malaysian soldier assigned to us for reasons only a suspicious government could think of, who, tripping over creepers and slinking through streams, always held his antique single-shot Browning across his chest; and I, who was not going to drag a film crew into the middle of Sarawak until I'd seen the nomadic Punan Dyaks, felt their bark-skin clothes and drunk their stout borak. But I hadn't thought about the Punans for two days because from the second we'd started trekking the soldier had shadowed the chief with his rifle, the safety off, looking to blow the chief's head off if he so much as sneezed.

At first I thought little of it. Malay officials distrusted natives, and owing to shameless logging and diamond exploration of native lands, feuds were fierce and longstanding. Aggressive tribesmen were sometimes found in forgotten jungle or washed up on outlying rivers with their throats slashed or bullets through their backs. Plus the issue of Asian soldiers and their guns. They flourish them on street corners, direct traffic with them, manage airport queues with them, sleep with them for all I knew. But we were miles into the tall trees, and the soldier kept stumbling because he would not for a second take his eyes off the chief, an unarmed man pushing sixty.

If you sketched a family tree for most inhabitants of North Borneo, you could trace their roots back to the jungle; so in spite of the stunt with his rifle, in a childish way the soldier seemed to revere the chief as a proper elder, fetching fronds for the chief's bed, giving him the first and biggest servings of rice. The chief, meanwhile, patiently fathered the soldier, showing him how to swing the machete, pointing out grim insects and critical herbage. Their minds addled by the nut, the young Ibans spat their mouthfuls and trudged on, heedless that their master was tracked point-blank.

For our third bivouac we chopped out the vines between the flutes of a towering banyan and slept in a partitioned circle, our heads to the trunk. Ten feet away the soldier had strung his rifle from a dangling liana. There was no wind and no rain. The cicadas were deafening, but I could hear the chief and the soldier chattering and laughing for an hour after we retired. To see the soldier stalking the chief by day and laughing with him by

night confounded me not so much as him leaving his wagon
where the chief could grab it and settle up for all his kinsmen
who'd refused to knuckle under.

Finally it was just the insects and the sound of my breath.
For a long time I studied the dark profile of the rifle, spinning
slowly, till I realized that the gun was empty, the shells in the
soldier's pocket. That only explained part of it, but enough for
me to sink into a doze.

We never saw grey sky through the tangled green roof but
rain was so long overdue we expected it. When it still hadn't
come the next morning, we arose early. I watched the soldier
untie his rifle from the liana and waited for him to thumb a shell
into the chamber. Instead he took up his vigil behind the chief,
who moved deftly along the intricate riverbank, the soldier
always stumbling an arm's length behind, his glare never leaving
the chief and his rifle held across his chest ready to extend fire.
That he carried on like this, with an empty gun, reduced him to a
rare kind of fool, a child lost in a deranged game of charades.

The leeches were getting bad, and I turned my thoughts back
to the Punan Dyaks, whose native turf loomed two hard days
away. Getting there was my job, I remained myself. A $300,000
documentary hinged on my contacting and getting some pictures
of the "savage" nomads, then stirring network television bosses
with tales of headhunting and scandalous rituals and all the
other bosh that might close the deal. But it was no good because
I'd thrashed to the edge of the world many times but never for
the stated reason of recounting documentaries, which were fund-
ed or not on the whim of maniacs. I was there, or told myself I
was there, to dig out my origins, believing that if I returned to a
place when people lived on equal terms with wood and water I
could answer blurry questions and learn to live on equal terms
with myself. But my hopes were dashed by this fool soldier
stalking an old man with an empty gun.

The others were getting ahead of me. I bitterly marched after
them.

The weather held and I noticed everyone (but the soldier)
stealing glances at the surrounding terrain, where beetling rock

outcrops soared in the ancient shade. The return of the monsoon was a concern, for the river could flood in minutes and force us into the spiked, squelchy hedgerow angling up sharply from the comparatively easy passage of the streambank.

In late afternoon we stopped for the night on a sandbar that curved with the river's sharp bight. It took the young Ibans and me thirty minutes to clear the scrub and limbs washed there during high water. Meanwhile the chief and the soldier, laughing and clowning, collected leaves and twigs for a fire in the lee of an ironwood trunk that we couldn't budge.

The young Ibans and I tumbled down the sandbar and spent an hour damming the river. But no fish ever came. When we clawed back up onto the sandbar I noticed the rifle laying on the ironwood trunk. For the hell of it I shouldered the old Browning, sighted at a distant rock and feigning to pull the trigger, sneered and yelled "BANG." The little moustache danced on the shoulder's lip. The soldier grabbed the rifle, flipped off the safety, shouldered it and pointing at the river, pulled the trigger. The thunderous report so startled me that I fell back onto the sand. The soldier and the Ibans laughed like hell. The chief didn't move, didn't say a word. I watched the soldier eject the spent cartridge, replace it with another from his pocket, flip the safety back on, then casually lay the rifle back onto the trunk, a tendril of smoke lofting off the band.

The soldier returned to the fire and on the chief's cue, apportioned us all servings of rice, big dollops of gluey gunk, the first and the biggest slid to the chief on a banana leaf. I cradled my heap of rice and took a seat on the hardwood trunk, one foot from the loaded rifle. The other, shoveling down rice with both hands, never looked up.

That night the soldier's snoring kept me awake, and I felt like grabbing the rifle and blowing his head off. I hated being laughed at. I hated the soldier's incomprehensible stalking. I hated the jungle and everyone in it.

The next morning it still hadn't rained so we broke camp shortly after sunup, eager to put some dry miles behind us. We could take a roundabout jungle thrash, or a direct route follow-

ing the riverbed through a steep gulch. The chief chose the
riverbed. We'd have to move fast for the march through the
gulch would take six hours, and if it started raining hard and fast
we'd get flooded out if we were not well along. As I made out in
my hack Melay, there was little escaping the gulch into the jungle — the terrain was too steep. The chief held up his hand vertically, nodded for effect, and I was hurled back to the Blue Nile.

There years before I'd filmed an early raft descent of the
"Blue." A week onto it, we took a wrong tributary and scram-
bled high onto a bordering crag to reckon our position. A flash
flood pinned us down on a ledge. An hour later and far below, a
wall of muddy water tore past, taking our rafts and a New
Zealand boatman along with it. It took us seventeen days to
thrash out to Embau. If it rained this time we wouldn't be walking, we'd be riding the muddy wave, just like the new Zealander.

We entered the gulch an hour later. Through overgrown walls
rose sheer from the river, the streambed was one hundred feet
across so I figured it would take a deluge several hours to fill the
canyon, or for the river to rise high enough to add to the scores
of logs teetering atop twenty-foot river boulders.

Shortly the walls closed in on both sides. Spangled with
dripping rep orchids, furry corkscrew vines spiraled down from
the heights, looping and crossing the shallow river then sweep-
ing back up the opposite wall. Dawn vapors crept up the lush
cliff sides to form a steamy nimbus, broken in spots to expose
the tight green mesh of canopy, two hundred feet overhead. The
air below us was thick and still and the river was low and barely
moved. We stopped.

The chief gave a short speech, his arms waving to one then
the other canyon wall. He emphasized words that I could not
understand. The soldier nodded quickly, many times, sweat
pouring down his bronzed face like a triton in a fountain. He
twice checked the safety on his rifle, making sure it was off. The
chief nodded, turned and resumed his march, his eyes traveling
between the canyon walls, the soldier's eyes burning holes
through his back.

The chief barked out and the soldier closed the distance between them to a rifle's length. I followed the soldier nearly as closely as he shadowed the chief, absorbed in a drama I did not understand. On both sides the young Ibans flanked out.

The chief stopped suddenly, raising one hand. The young Ibans froze but the soldier jumped and for the first time, moved the rifle away from his chest. His knees flexed. His face was twisted from tension and awe. Since violence is essentially wordless, it follows that it can find play only when communication breaks down. And since the soldier had said nothing for several hours and looked ready to shoulder his rifle and blast the chief into the next world, I thought the time had come. I had long given up trying to make any sense of this, and in my frustration and anger, and terror of getting flushed out of the gulch, I almost wanted the soldier to shoot, to do *something* the shatter the tension. But the chief dropped his gaze from high on the righthand wall, lowered his arms and marched on. The soldier brought the rifle back across his chest and fell into file.

The heat and humidity hung on us like a curse. I tramped on, drunk with adrenaline, staring at the soldier. It had turned into a game with me, not believing and yet expecting to see a man shot in the back. I imagined the chief floating face down in the river. I imagined worse things and was perfectly taken by it all. It was my only way to ignore the thin drizzle bleeding through the canopy. Our hours were numbered.

The chief's attention returned to the cliff sides as they gently eased in angle. For a moment I tore my eyes away from the soldier and panned up the left wall, which looked like the same verdant brawl from waterline to gray sky. Meanwhile the chief weaved silently, and carefully moved from shadow to shadow. Off to each side the young Ibans did the same. The soldier's face was twisted up again. When he stumbled, the chief shot him a glance that I though would cost the chief, but the soldier only nodded. His rifle shook in his hands and I didn't care. A copper taste hung on my tongue and I wanted to shout. The river had risen a foot and in spots covered most of the riverbed. The young Ibans and I were jogging, then holding up for the chief and the soldier, then jogging again. Whatever the chief was up to, the Iban's didn't like it any more than I did. I wanted to get the hell out of that canyon in one piece, but we couldn't jog anymore because the water was now knee deep.

We moved into a cut of sunlight. The chief treaded lightly along a spit of gravel, three creeping shadows playing across the still water to our left. For several minutes the chief's gaze had lingered high upon the righthand wall. With a last step so slow it took some balance to perform, the chief's hand came up; with his eyes still riveted up and right, he froze. The soldier froze. Spread out on both sides, the young Iban's froze. I froze, and could feel my heartbeat in my hands and could hear it in my ears.

The chief wheeled around. The soldier extended the rifle at arm's length, one hand clasping the middle of the barrel, the other, the very butt of the stock. In one motion the chief snatched the rifle, shouldered it, turned and no sooner had the barrel settled on a spot high on the righthand wall than a yellow flash leaped from the muzzle as the report banged off the canyon walls, bandied up and out through the holes in the thinning canopy. A dark object began rolling down the wall, tumbling with greater and greater speed. I finally locked onto it as it plunged over a last ceiling and splashed into a pool one hundred feet away.

I spun to face the chief but he had already wandered off downstream, his eyes probing high on the left wall. The young soldier fumbled to thumb a new shell into the chamber, fumbled mainly because he kept looking up to see how far the chief had advanced. Gun loaded, safety off, the soldier scampered after and took up his position, walking quietly and in step behind the chief.

In ten minutes the storm shot through the canopy like a blast from a fire hose and the five of us ran when we could, sometimes clawing along the edge of the cliff when the river ran deep, other times fording and even swimming in the swelling current. The river pumped. Quantities of trees and mud joined the flow. When the ravine opened up and hour later we'd been bodysurfing a waist-deep torrent for ten minutes and were barked and bashed all over. The young Ibans had lost the deer and the soldier had lost his old Browning rifle. We were sad about that.

A LEAP
IN THE DARK

by Charles A. Lindbergh

"I took off from Lambert (St. Louis) Field, September 16, 1926, at 4:25 p.m., and after an uneventful trip, arrived at Peoria, Illinois, at 5:55 p.m. I left Peoria Field at 6:10 p.m. in a light ground haze, though the sky was practically clear.

Darkness fell about twenty-five miles northeast of Peoria and I took up a compass course, checking on the lights of the town below, until a low fog rolled in under me a few miles northeast of Marseilles and the Illinois River. The fog extended from the ground up to about six hundred feet and, as I was unable to fly under it, I turned back and attempted to drop a flare and land. But the flare was a dud and I again headed for Maywood, hoping to find a break in the fog over the field. I was confused about the flare failure, and in rummaging around the cockpit I discovered that the release lever was too short. I yanked out a little more cable on the release device and resolved to try to drop the flare a second time.

I continued on a compass course of fifty degrees until 7:15 p.m., when I saw a dull glow on the top of the fog, indicating a town below. Several of these light patches glowed atop the thick fog—visible only when looking away from the moon—and I knew them to be towns bordering the Maywood Field. At no time, however, was I able to locate the exact position of the field, although I understood that searchlights were directed upward and two barrels of gasoline had been ignited to attract my attention.

Several times I descended to the top of the fog, which according to my altimeter was eight to nine hundred feet high. Excepting scattered clouds, the sky above was clear, the moon and stars shining brightly and hurling their light on the crown of the somber cloudbank.

I circled around for thirty-five minutes, but it was no good. Fuel was running seriously low, so I headed west, hoping to clear Lake Michigan and, eventually, to pick up one of the lights on the transcontinental line. After flying west for fifteen minutes and seeing no break in the fog, I turned southwest; with luck I might clear the edge of the fog south of the Illinois River. I'd been circling around for over two hours now.

At 8:20 p.m., my motor cut out. I frantically dialed on the reserve tank. I was only 1,500 feet high and, as the motor did not pick up as soon as I expected, I shoved the flashlight into my belt and was about to release the parachute flare and bail when the engine finally hacked back to life. The main tank was dry. I was down to twenty minutes flying-time. Maximum.

There were no openings on the fog and I decided to leave the ship as soon as the reserve tank was spent. I tried to get the mail pit open, with the idea of throwing out the mail sacks and then jumping, but was unable to open the front buckle.

I knew that the risk of fire, with no gasoline in the tanks, was very slight, so I began to climb for altitude when through a small rent in the clouds, I saw a flicker light on the ground. This was the first light I had seen for over two hours and, as almost enough gasoline for fifteen minutes flying remained in the reserve, I glided down to twelve hundred feet and pulled out the flare-release cable, as nearly as I could judge over the spot where the light had appeared. This time the flare worked, but only to illuminate the top of a solid bank of fog, into which the flare disappeared like an anchor dropped into a black sea.

Seven minutes' gasoline remained in the gravity tank. Seeing the glow of a town through the fog, I turned towards open country and nosed the plane up. At 5,000 feet the motor sputtered and died. There were no more options. I unbuckled, stepped up on the cowling and out over the right side of the cockpit, and bailed, pulling the rip-cord after about a hundred-foot fall. The parachute, an Irvin seat-service type, functioned perfectly; I was falling head downward when the risers jerked me into an upright position and the chute opened.

I pulled the flashlight from my belt and was playing it down towards the top of the fogbank when I heard the plane's motor pick up. When I jumped, the motor had stopped dead and I'd neglected to cut the switches. Apparently, when the ship nosed down, the last dregs of gasoline had drained down to the carburetor. Presently the ship came into sight, about a quarter-mile away and heading directly for me. I put the flashlight in a pocket of my flying suit, preparatory to slippig the parachute out of the way if necessary. The plane was making a left spiral of about a mile diameter and passed approximately three hundred yards away from my chute, leaving me on the outside of the circle.

I couldn't tell which—the plane, or I—was descending more rapidly, and yanking on the lines, tried to glide my chute away from the spiral path of the ship.

The ship passed out of sight, but reappeared again in a few seconds. Now I could see that the ship and I were descending at precisely the same rate of speed. I counted five spirals, each one a little closer, until during the last pass the ship roared by so close the propwash partially collapsed my chute and I fell like a stone before the canopy again blossomed out and I settled back into fluid descent. Then I pierced the fog-bank and could see nothing.

I knew that the ground was within 1,000 feet and I reached for the flashlight, but it was gone. I could see neither earth nor stars and had no idea what kind of territory was below. I crossed my legs to keep from straddling a branch or wire, guarded my face with my hands and waited. Then I heard the coughing din of the engine and knew the ship was circling back my way. Lofting down through an impenetrable fog bank, knowing my ship was grinding directly toward me, caused in me a sensation I won't try to describe. Precisely how close the ship came I do not know because I couldn't see my hand in front of my face; but the screaming engine and the buffeting of my chute said I'd been a lucky man indeed.

Presently I saw the outline of the ground and a moment later crashed into a cornfield. The corn was over my head and the chute was lying on top of the cornstalks. I hurriedly packed it and started down a corn row. The ground visibility was about one hundred yards.

In a few minutes I came to a stubble field and some wagon tracks, which I followed to a farmyard a quarter-mile away. After reaching the farmyard, I noticed auto headlights and a spotlight playing over the roadside. Thinking that someone might have located the wreck of the plane, I walked over to the car. The occupants asked whether I had heard an airplane crash and it required some time to explain to them that I had been piloting the plane and was searching for it myself. I had to display the parachute as evidence before they believed me. The farmer was sure, as were most others in a three-mile radius, that the ship had just missed his house and crashed near-by. In fact, he could locate within a few rods the spot where he heard it hit the ground, and we spent an unsuccessful quarter-hour hunting for the wreck in that vicinity before going to the farmhouse to arrange for a searching party and telephone St. Louis and Chicago.

I had just put in the long-distance calls when the phone rang and we were notified that the plane had been found in a cornfield over two miles away.

It took several minutes to reach the site of the crash, due to the necessity of slow driving through the fog. A small crowd had already assembled when we arrived.

The plane was wound up in a ball-shaped mass. It had narrowly missed one farmhouse and had hooked its left wing in a grain shack a quarter-mile beyond. The ship had landed on the left wing and wheel and had skidded along the ground for eighty yards, going through one fence before coming to rest in the edge of a cornfield, about a hundred yards short of a barn. The mail pit was laid open and one sack of mail was on the ground. The ship was history. The mail however, was uninjured."

ANNAPURNA

by Maurice Herzog

The French ascent of Annapurna was the first ascent of the mountain; the first ascent of an eight-thousand-meter peak, a feat attempted over thirty times by parties of various nations; the first successful French Himalayan expedition; and the last time leader Maurice Herzog would ever climb. The following piece, excerpted from Herzog's classic *Annapurna*, describes the epic ascent and descent of one of history's greatest climbs by four of the heroic names in the sport: Louis Lachanel, Lionel Terray, Gaston Rébuffat and leader, Maurice Herzog. Their ascent was unprecedented, likewise the fact that they ever made it there. The entire area was so remote and uncharted that over a month was required in discovering a passage to reach the mountain at all, to say nothing of finding a possible route to the summit. Consequently their final assault was a desperate race against time, for the team had to be off the mountain before the onslaught of the pending monsoon.

After battling through avalanches and cold so horrendous that "it absolutely perished me" (according to Terray), Herzog and partner Louis "Biscante" Lachanel summited on June 3, 1950. The victory cost both climbers dearly. Months later, in the American Hospital at Neuilly, France, Herzog dictated "the story of a terrible adventure that we survived only by an incredible series of miracles." Told in a straightforward style tempered with the gallant decorum of the era, *Annapurna* remains the quintessential mountaineering epic, unsurpassed in power and effect. Here we join Herzog and Lachanel at Camp V, at an altitude of 24,600 feet. Several days prior, savage winds and swirling snow had thwarted Terray and Rébuffat on the first summit bid, and the two, frozen and spent, had since retreated from Camp V to a lower camp.

On the third of June 1950, first light found us still clinging to the tent poles at Camp V. Gradually the wind abated, and died away altogether. I made desperate attempts to push back the soft, icy stuff that stifled me. My mental powers were numbed, and we did not exchange a single word.

To everyone who reached it, Camp V became one of the worst memories of his life. We had only one thought; to get away. We should have waited, but at half past five, we felt we couldn't stick it out any longer.

"Let's go," I muttered. "Can't stay here a minute longer."

"Yes, let's go," repeated Lachanel.

It was quite hard enough work to get ourselves and our boots out of our sleeping bags—and the boots were frozen stiff so that we got them on only with the greatest difficulty. Every movement made us terribly breathless. Our gaiters were stiff as a board, and I succeeded in lacing mine up; Lachanel couldn't manage his.

"No need for the rope, eh, Biscante?"

"No need."

That was two pounds saved. I pushed a tube of condensed milk, some nougat and a pair of socks into my sack. The camera was loaded with a black and white film; I had a color film in reserve.

We went outside and put on our crampons, which we kept on all day. We wore as many clothes as possible; our sacks were very light. At six o'clock we started off. It was brilliantly fine, but also very cold. Our crampons bit deep into the steep slopes of ice and hard snow, up which lay the first stage of our climb.

Later the slope became slightly less steep and more uniform. Sometimes the hard crust bore our weight, but at others we broke through and sank into soft powder snow, which made progress exhausting. We took turns in making the track and often stopped without any word having passed between us. My mind was working very slowly, and I was perfectly aware of the low state of my intelligence. It was easiest just to stick to one thought at a time. Safest, too. The cold was penetrating. For all our special eiderdown clothing we felt as though we'd nothing on. Whenever we halted, we stamped our feet. Lachanel went as far as to take off one boot that was a bit tight; he was in terror of frostbite.

"I don't want to be like Lambert," he said. Raymond Lambert, a Geneva guide, had to have all his toes amputated after an eventful climb during which he got his feet frostbitten.

While Lachanel rubbed his feet, I looked at the summits of Dhaulagiri. The complicated structure of these mountains, with which our many laborious explorations had made us familiar, was now spread out plainly at our feet.

The going was incredibly exhausting, and every step was a struggle of mind over matter. We came out into the sunlight and Lachanel continued to complain of his feet. "I can't feel anything. I think I'm beginning to get frostbite." And once again, he undid his boot.

I began to be seriously worried. I knew from experience how insidiously and quickly frostbite can set in. Nor was Lachenal under any illusions.

"We're in danger of having frozen feet. Do you think it's worth it?"

This was most disturbing. It was my responsibility as leader to think of the others. There was no doubt about frostbite being a very real danger. Did Annapurna justify such risks?

Lachenal had laced his boots up again, and once more we continued to force our way through the snow. The whole of the Sickle glacier was now in view, bathed in light. We still had a long way to go to cross it, and then there was the rock band. Would we find a gap in it?

My feet, like Lachenal's, were very cold; and I continued to wriggle my toes, even when we were moving. I could not feel them, but that was nothing new in the mountains, and if I kept on moving them, it would keep the circulation going.

Lachenal appeared to me as a sort of specter; he was alone in his world, I in mine. But—and this was odd enough—any effort was slightly less exhausting than lower down. Perhaps it was hope lending us wings. Even through dark glasses the snow was blinding, the sun beating straight down on the ice. We looked down upon precipitous ridges, which dropped away into space, and upon tiny glaciers far, far below. Familiar peaks soared arrowlike into the sky. Suddenly Lachenal grabbed me and asked, "If I go back, what will you do?"

A whole sequence of pictures flashed through my head; the days of marching in sweltering heat, the hard pitches we had overcome, the tremendous efforts we had all made to lay siege to the mountain, the daily heroism of all my friends in establishing the camps. In an hour or two, perhaps, victory would be ours. Must we give up? My whole being revolted against the idea. I had made up my mind, irrevocably. Today we were consecrating an idea, and no sacrifice was too great.

"I should go on by myself."

If he wished to go down it was not for me to stop him.

"Then I'll follow you."

I was no longer anxious. Nothing could stop us now from getting to the top. The psychological atmosphere changed with these few words, and we went forward now as brothers.

I had the strangest and most vivid impressions, such as I had never before known in the mountains. There was something unnatural in the way I saw Lachenal and everything around us. I smiled to myself at the paltriness of our efforts, for I could stand apart and watch myself making these efforts. But all sense of exertion was gone, as though there were no longer any gravity. This diaphanous landscape, this quintessence of purity—these were not the mountains I knew, rather the mountains of my dreams.

The snow, sprinkled over every rock and gleaming in the sun, was radiant. I had never seen such complete transparency and I was living in a world of crystal. Sounds were indistinct, the atmosphere like cotton wool.

An enormous gulf was between me and the world. This was a different universe — withered, deserted, lifeless; a fantastic universe where the presence of man was not foreseen, perhaps not desired.

The summit ridge drew nearer, and we reached the foot of the ultimate rock band. The slope was very steep and the snow interspersed with rocks.

"Couloir!"

The whispered word from one to another indicated the key to the rocks—the last line of defense.

"What luck!"

The couloir up the rocks, though steep, was feasible.

The sky was sapphire blue. With great effort we edged over to the right, avoiding the rock; we preferred to keep to the snow on account of our crampons, and it was not long before we set foot in the couloir. It was fairly steep, and we had a minute's hesitation. Should we have enough strength left to overcome this final obstacle?

Fortunately the snow was hard, and by kicking steps we were able to manage, thanks to our crampons. A false move would have been fatal. There was no need to make handholds; our axes, driven in as far as possible, served as anchors.

Lachenal went splendidly. It was a hard struggle here, but he kept going. Lifting our eyes occasionally from the slope, we saw the couloir opening out on to . . . well, we didn't quite know, probably a ridge. But where was the top, left or right? Stopping at every step and leaning on our axes, we tried to recover our breath and to calm down our racing hearts. We knew we were there now — that nothing could stop us. No need to exchange looks — each of us would have read the same determination in the other's eyes. A slight detour to the left, a few more steps. The summit ridge came gradually nearer; a few rocks to avoid. We dragged ourselves up. Could we possibly be there?

Yes!

A fierce and savage wind tore at us.

We were on top of Annapurna! 8,075 meters, 26,493 feet.

Our hearts overflowed with unspeakable happiness.

"If only the others could know . . . "

If only everyone could know!

The summit was a corniced crest of ice; and the precipices on the far side plunged vertically down beneath us, concealing the gentle, fertile valley of Pokhara, 23,000 feet below. Above us there was nothing!

Our mission was accomplished. But at the same time we had accomplished something infinitely greater. How wonderful life would now become! What an inconceivable experience it is to attain one's ideal and, at the very same moment, to fulfill oneself. Never had I felt happiness like this, so intense and yet so pure. That brown rock, the highest of them all, that ridge of ice—were these the goals of a lifetime? Or were they, rather, the limits of man's pride?

"Well, what about going down?"

Lachenal's words shook me. What were his own feelings? Did he simply think he had finished another climb, as in the Alps? Did he think one could just go down again like that, with nothing more to it?

"One minute! I must take some photographs."

"Hurry up!"

I fumbled feverishly in my sack, pulled out the camera, took out the little French flag that was right at the bottom, and the pennants. Useless gestures, no doubt, but something more than symbols—eloquent tokens of affection and goodwill. I tied the strips of material—stained by sweat and by the food in the sacks—to the shaft of my ice-ax, the only flagstaff at hand. Then I focused my camera on Lachenal.

"Now, will you take me?"

"Hand it over! Hurry up!" said Lachenal.

He took several pictures and then handed me back the camera. I loaded a color film and we repeated the process to be certain of bringing back records to be cherished in the future.

"Are you mad?" asked Lachenal. "We haven't a minute to lose; we must go down at once."

And in fact, a glance round showed me that the weather was no longer gloriously fine, as it had been in the morning. Lachenal was fiendishly impatient.

"We must go down!"

His was the reaction of the mountaineer who knows his own domain. But I just could not accustom myself to the idea that we had won our victory.

It was impossible to build a cairn. There were no stones; everything was frozen. Lachenal stamped his feet; he felt them freezing. I felt mine freezing too, but paid little attention. The highest mountain to be climbed by man lay under our feet! The names of our predecessors on these heights raced through my mind: Mummery, Mallory and Irvine, Bauer, Welzenbach, Tilman, Shipton. How many of them were dead? How many had found on these mountains what, to them, was the finest end of all?

"Come on, straight down," called Lachenal.

He had already done up his sack and had started going down. I took out my pocket aneroid: 8,500 meters. I smiled. I swallowed a little condensed milk and left the tube behind—the only trace of my passage. I did up my sack, put on my gloves and my glasses, seized my ice-ax. One look around and I, too, hurried down the slope. Before disappearing into the couloir I gave one last look at the summit, which would henceforth be all our joy and all our consolation.

Lachenal was already far below; he had reached the foot of the couloir. I hurried down in his tracks. At every step, one had to take care that the snow did not break away beneath one's weight. Lachenal, going faster than I thought he was capable of, was now on the long traverse. It was my turn to cross the area of

mixed rock and snow. At last I reached the foot of the rockband.
I had hurried and I was out of breath. I undid my sack. What had
I been going to do? I couldn't remember.

"My gloves!"

Before I had time to bend over, I saw them slide and roll.
Stunned, I watched them rolling down slowly, with no appearance of stopping. The movement of those gloves was engraved
in my sight as something irredeemable.

"Quickly! Down to Camp Five."

Rébuffat and Terray would be there. My concern dissolved
like magic. I now had a fixed objective again; to reach the camp.
Never for a minute did it occur to me to use as gloves the socks
that I always carry in reserve for just such a mishap as this.

On I went, trying to catch up with Lachenal. It had been two
o'clock when we reached the summit. We had started out at six
in the morning, but I had lost all sense of time. I felt as though I
were running, whereas in fact I was walking normally, perhaps
rather slowly, and I had to keep stopping to get my breath. The
sky was now covered with gray, dirty-looking clouds. An icy
wind sprang up. We must push on! But where was Lachenal? I
spotted him a couple of hundred yards away, looking as though
he was never going to stop.

The clouds grew thicker and came down over us; the wind
blew stronger, but I did not suffer from the cold. Perhaps the
descent had restored my circulation. Should I be able to find the
tents in the mist? I watched the rib ending in the beaklike point
that overlooked the camp. It was gradually swallowed up by the
clouds, but I was able to make out the spearhead rib lower down.
If the mist should thicken, I would make straight for that rib and
follow it down, and in this way I should be bound to come upon
the tent.

Lachenal disappeared from time to time, and then the mist
was so thick that I lost sight of him altogether. I kept going as
fast as my breathing would allow.

The slope was now steeper; a few patches of bare ice followed the smooth stretches of snow. A good sign! I was nearing
the camp. How difficult to find one's way in thick mist! I kept

the course I had set by the steepest angle of the slope. With my crampons I went straight down walls of bare ice. There were some patches ahead, a few more steps. It was the camp all right, but there were two tents!

So Rébuffat and Terray had come up. What a mercy!

I got there, dropping down from above. The platform had been extended, and the two tents were facing each other. I tripped over one of the guy-ropes of the first tent. There was movement inside; Rébuffat and Terray put their heads out.

"We've made it! We're back from Annapurna!"

Rébuffat and Terray received the news with great excitement.

"But what about Biscante?" asked Terray anxiously.

"He won't be long. He was just in front of me! What a day—started out at six this morning—didn't stop . . . got up at last."

Words failed me. The sight of familiar faces dispelled the strange feeling that I had experienced since morning, and I became, once more, just a mountaineer.

Terray, who was speechless with delight, wrung my hands. Then the smile vanished from his face: "Maurice—your hands!" There was an uneasy silence. I had forgotten that I had lost my gloves; my fingers were violet and hard as wood. The two stared at them in dismay. Still floating on a sea of joy, remote from reality, I leaned over toward Terray and said confidentially, "You're in such splendid form, and you've done so marvelously, it's absolutely tragic you didn't come up there with us!"

"What I did was for the expedition, and anyway, you've got up, and that's a victory for the whole lot of us."

The rapture I had felt on the summit had been transformed by his words into a complete and perfect joy with no shadow upon it. His answer proved that this victory was not just one man's achievement, a matter for personal pride; no—and Terray was the first to understand this—it was a victory for us all, a victory for mankind itself.

"Hi! Help! Help!"

"Biscante!" exclaimed the others.

Still half-intoxicated, I had heard nothing. Terray's thoughts flew to his partner on so many unforgettable climbs. Together they had so often skirted death and won so many splendid victories. Putting his head out, and seeing Lachenal clinging to the slope a hundred yards lower down, he dressed in frantic haste.

Out he went. But Lachenal had disappeared. Terray could only utter unintelligible cries. A violent wind sent the mist tearing by. Under the stress of emotion Terray had not realized how it falsified distances.

"Biscante! Biscante!"

He had spotted him through a rift in the mist, lying on the slope much lower down than he had thought. Terray glissaded down like a madman. How would he be able to brake without crampons, on the wind-hardened snow? But Terray was a first-class skier, and with a jump turn he stopped beside Lachenal, who was suffering from a concussion after his tremendous fall. In a state of collapse, with no ice ax, balaclava, or gloves, and only one crampon, he gazed vacantly around him.

"My feet are frostbitten. Take me down so that Oudot can see to me."

"It can't be done," said Terray sorrowfully. "Can't you see we're in the middle of a storm? It'll be dark soon."

But Lachenal was obsessed by the fear of amputation. He tore the ax out of Terray's hands and tried to force his way down; but soon saw the futility of his action and resolved to climb up to the camp. While Terray cut steps without stopping, Lachenal, ravaged and exhausted as he was, dragged himself along on all fours.

Meanwhile, I had gone into Rébuffat's tent. He was appalled at the sight of my hands and, as rather incoherently I told him what we had done, he took a piece of rope and began flicking my fingers. Then he took off my boots with great difficulty, for my feet were swollen, and beat my feet and rubbed them. We soon heard Terray giving Lachenal the same treatment in the other tent.

Outside, the storm howled and the snow was still falling. The mist grew thick and darkness came. As on the previous night, we had to cling to the poles to prevent the tents being carried away by the wind. The only two air mattresses were given to Lachenal and myself, while Terray and Rébuffat both sat on ropes, rucksacks, and provisions to keep themselves off the snow. They rubbed, slapped, and beat us with a rope. Sometimes the blows fell on the living flesh, and howls arose from both tents. Rébuffat persevered; it was essential to continue, painful as it was. Gradually life returned to my feet as well as to my hands. Lachenal, too, found that feeling was returning.

Now Terray summoned up the energy to prepare some hot drinks. He called to Rébuffat that he would pass him a mug, so two hands stretched out toward each other between the two tents and were instantly covered with snow. The liquid was boiling, though scarcely more than 60 degrees centigrade (140 degrees Fahrenheit). I swallowed it greedily and felt infinitely better.

The night was absolute hell. Frightful wind battered us incessantly while the never-ceasing snow piled up on the tents.

"Rébuffat! Gaston! Gaston!"

I recognized Terray's voice.

"Time to be off!"

I heard the sounds without grasping their meaning. Was it light already? I was not in the least surprised that the other two had given up all thought of going to the top, and I did not at all grasp the measure of their sacrifice.

Outside, the storm redoubled in violence. The tent shook and the fabric flapped alarmingly. It had usually been fine in the mornings: Did this mean the monsoon was upon us?

"Gaston! Are you ready?" Terray called again.

"One minute," answered Rébuffat. He had to put my boots on and do everything to get me ready. I let myself be handled like a baby. In the other tent Terray finished dressing Lachenal, whose feet were still swollen and would not fit into his boots. So Terray gave him his own, which were bigger. To get Lachenal's onto his own feet, he had to make slits in them. As a precaution he put a sleeping bag and some food into his sack and shouted to us to do the same. Were his words lost in the storm? Or were we too intent on leaving this hellish place to listen to his instructions?

Lachenal and Terray were already outside.

"We're going down!" they shouted.

Then Rébuffat tied me on the rope and we went out. There were only two ice axes for the four of us, so Rébuffat and Terray took them as a matter of course. For a moment as we left the two tents of Camp V, I felt ashamed at leaving all this good equipment behind.

Already the first rope seemed a long way down below us. We were blinded by the squalls of snow and we could not hear each other a yard away. Ahead of us the other two were losing no time. Lachenal went first and, safeguarded by Terray, he forced the pace in his anxiety to get down. There were no tracks to show us the way, but it was engraved on all our minds—straight down the slope for 400 yards, then traverse to the left for 150 to 200 yards to get to Camp IV.

The snow stuck to our cagoules and turned us into white phantoms noiselessly flitting against a background equally white. We began to sink in dreadfully, nothing worse for bodies already on the edge of exhaustion.

Were we too high or too low? No one could tell. The snow was in a dangerous condition, but we did not seem to realize it. We were forced to admit that we were not on the right route, so we retraced our steps and climbed up above the serac that overhung us. No doubt, we decided, we should be on the right level now. With Rébuffat leading, we went back over the way that had cost us such an effort. I followed him jerkily, saying nothing, and determined to go on to the end. If Rébuffat had fallen, I could never have held him.

We went doggedly on from one serac to another. Each time we thought we had recognized the right route, and each time there was a fresh disappointment. If only the mist would lift, if only the snow would stop for a second! On the slope it seemed to be growing deeper every minute. Only Terray and Rébuffat were capable of breaking the trail, and they relieved each other at regular intervals, without a word and without a second's hesitation.

I admired this determination of Rébuffat's, for which he is so justly famed. He did not intend to die! With desperation and superhuman effort he forged ahead. The slowness of his progress would have dismayed even the most obstinate climber, but he would not give up, and in the end the mountain yielded to his perseverance.

Terray, when his turn came, charged madly ahead. He was like a force of nature. His physical strength was exceptional, his willpower no less remarkable. Lachenal gave him considerable trouble. Perhaps he was not quite in his right mind. He said it was no use going on; we must dig a hole in the snow and wait for fine weather. He swore at Terray and called him a madman. Nobody but Terray would have been capable of dealing with him—he just tugged sharply on the rope, and Lachenal was forced to follow.

We were well and truly lost.

Camp IV was certainly on the left, on the edge of the Sickle. On that point we were all agreed. But the wall of ice that gave it such magnificent protection now hid the tents from us. In mist like this we should have been right on top of them before we spotted them.

Perhaps if we called, someone would hear us. Lachenal gave the signal, but snow absorbs sound, and his shout seemed to carry only a few yards. All four of us called out together, "One . . . two . . . three . . . help!"

We got the impression that our united shout carried a long way, so we began again. Not a sound in reply!

Now and again Terray took off his boots and rubbed his feet; the sight of our frostbitten limbs had made him aware of the danger, and he had the strength of mind to do something about it. Like Lachenal, he was haunted by the idea of amputation. For me it was too late; my feet and hands, already affected from yesterday, were beginning to freeze up again.

Night had suddenly fallen, and it was essential to come to a decision without wasting another minute. If we remained on the slope, we should be dead before the morning. We would have to bivouac. What the conditions would be like were anyone's guess, for we all knew what it meant to bivouac above 23,000 feet.

With his ax Terray began to dig a hole. Lachenal went over to a snow-filled crevasse a few yards farther on, then suddenly let out a yell and disappeared before our eyes. We stood helpless: Would we, or rather would Terray and Rébuffat, have enough strength needed to get him out? The crevasse was completely blocked up save for the one little hole that Lachenal had fallen through.

"Lachenal!" called Terray.

A voice, muffled by many thicknesses of ice and snow, came up to us. It was impossible to make out what he was saying.

"Lachenal!"

"I'm here!"

"Anything broken?"

"No! It'll do for the night! Come along."

This shelter was heaven-sent. None of us would have had the strength to dig a hole big enough to protect the lot of us from the wind. Without hesitation Terray let himself drop into the crevasse, and a loud "Come on!" told us he had arrived safely. In my turn I let myself go: It was a regular toboggan slide. I shot down a sort of twisting tunnel, very steep, and about thirty feet long. I came out at great speed into the opening beyond and was literally hurled to the bottom of the crevasse. We let Rébuffat know he could come, by giving a tug on the rope.

The intense cold of this minute grotto shriveled us up; the enclosing walls of ice were damp and the floor a carpet of fresh snow. By huddling together there was just room for the four of us. Icicles hung from the ceiling, and we broke some of them off to make more headroom and kept little bits to suck—it was a long time since we had had anything to drink.

At least for the night we should be protected from the wind, and the temperature would remain fairly even, though the damp was extremely unpleasant. We settled ourselves in the dark as best we could. As always in a bivouac, we took off our boots; without this precaution the constriction would cause immediate frostbite. Terray unrolled the sleeping bag that he had had the foresight to bring, and settled himself in relative comfort. We put on everything warm that we had and huddled up close to each other in our search for a hypothetical position in which the warmth of our bodies could be combined without loss. But we couldn't keep still for a second.

Terray generously tried to give me part of his sleeping bag. He had understood the seriousness of my condition and knew why it was that I said nothing and remained quite passive; he realized that I had abandoned all hope for myself. He massaged me for nearly two hours; his feet, too, might have frozen, but he didn't appear to give the matter a thought. He was doing so much to help me that it would have been ungrateful of me not to go on struggling to live. Though my heart was like a lump of ice, I was astonished to be quite clear in my thoughts, and yet I floated in a kind of peaceful happiness. There was still a breath of life in me, but it dwindled steadily as the hours went by. Terray's massage no longer had any effect upon me. It was all over. Wasn't this cavern the most beautiful grave I could hope for? Death caused me no grief, no regret—I smiled at the thought.

After hours of torpor a voice mumbled, "Daylight!"

This made some impression on the others. I only felt surprised—I had not thought that daylight would penetrate so far down.

"Too early to start," said Rébuffat.

A ghastly light spread through our grotto, and we could vaguely make out the shapes of each other's heads. A queer noise from a long way off came down to us—a sort of prolonged hiss. The noise increased. Suddenly I was buried, blinded, smothered beneath an avalanche of new snow. The icy snow spread over the cavern, finding its way through every gap in our clothing. I ducked my head between my knees and covered myself with both arms. The snow flowed on and on. There was a terrible silence. We were not completely buried, but there was snow everywhere. We got up, taking care not to bang our heads against the ceiling of ice, and tried to shake ourselves. We were all in our stocking feet in the snow. The first thing to do was to find our boots.

Rébuffat and Terray began to search, and realized at once that they were blind. Yesterday they had taken off their glasses to lead us down and now they were paying for it. Lachenal was the first to lay hands upon a pair of boots. He tried to put them on, but they were Rébuffat's. Rébuffat attempted to climb up the chute down which we had come yesterday and that the avalanche had followed in its turn.

"Hi, Gaston! What's the weather like?" called up Terray.

"Can't see a thing. It's blowing hard."

We were still groping for our things. Terray found his boots and put them on awkwardly, unable to see what he was doing.

At the bottom of the crevasse there were still two of us looking for our boots. Lachenal poked fiercely with an ice ax. I was calmer and tried to proceed more rationally. We extracted crampons and an ax in turn from the snow, but still no boots.

There was very little room; we were bent double and got in each other's way. Lachenal decided to go out without his boots. He called frantically, hauled himself up on the rope, trying to get a hold or to wiggle his way up, digging his toes into the snow walls. Terray from outside pulled as hard as he could. I watched him go; he gathered speed and disappeared.

When he emerged from the opening he saw the sky was clear and blue, and he began to run like a madman, shrieking, "It's fine, it's fine!"

I set to work again to search the cave. The boots had to be found, or Lachenal and I were done for. On all fours, with nothing on my hands or feet, I raked the snow, stirring it around this way and that, hoping every second to come upon something hard. I was no longer capable of thinking. I reacted like an animal fighting for its life.

I found one boot! The other was tied to it—a pair! Having ransacked the whole cave, I at last found the other pair. There was no question of putting my boots on—my hands were like lumps of wood and I could hold nothing in my fingers; my feet were very swollen—I should never be able to get boots on them. I twisted the rope around the boots as well as I could and called up the chute, "Lionel . . . boots!"

There was no answer, but he must have heard, for with a jerk the precious boots shot up. Soon after, the rope came down again. My turn. I pulled myself out by clutching Terray's legs; he was just about all in, and I was in the last stages of exhaustion. Terray was close to me and I whispered, "Lionel . . . I'm dying!"

He supported me and helped me away from the crevasse. Lachenal and Rébuffat were sitting in the snow a few yards away. The instant Lionel let go of me I sank down and dragged myself along on all fours.

The weather was perfect. Quantities of snow had fallen the day before and the mountains were magnificent.

I knew the end was near, but it was the end that all mountaineers wish for—an end in keeping with their ruling passion. I was grateful to the mountains for being so beautiful for me that day, and as awed by their silence as if I had been in church. I was in no pain, and had no worry. My utter calmness was alarming. Terray came staggering toward me, and I told him, "It's all over for me. Go on . . . you have a chance. You must take it . . . over to the left . . . that's the way."

I felt better after telling him that. But Terray would have none of it. "We'll help you. If we get away, so will you."

At this moment Lachenal shouted, "Help! Help!"

Obviously he didn't know what he was doing . . . or did he? He was the only one of the four of us who could see Camp IV down below. Perhaps his calls would be heard. They were shrieks of despair; we were lost.

I joined in with the others. "One . . . two . . . three . . . help!"
The noise I made was more of a whisper than a shout. Terray
insisted that I should put my boots on, but my hands were dead.
Neither our shouts nor Terray, who was unable to see, could help
much, so I said to Lachenal, "Come and help me to put my
boots on."

"Don't be silly. We must go on."

And off he went once again in the wrong direction, straight
down.

Terray resolutely got out his knife, and with fumbling hands
slit the uppers of my boots back and front. Split in two like this I
could get them on, but it was not easy, and I had to make several
attempts. Soon I lost heart. What was the use of it all anyway,
since I was going to stay where I was? But Terray pulled violently and finally he succeeded. He laced up my now gigantic
boots, missing half the hooks. But how was I going to walk with
my stiff joints?

"To the left, Lionel!"

"You're crazy, Maurice," said Lachenal, "It's to the right,
straight down."

Terray did not know what to think of these conflicting views.
He had not given up like me—he was going to fight—but what,
at the moment, could he do? The three of them discussed which
way to go.

I remained sitting in the snow. Gradually my mind lost its
grip. I let myself drift. I saw pictures of shady slopes, peaceful
paths, there was a scent of resin. I was going to die in my own
mountains. My body had no feeling. Everything was frozen.

"Aah . . . aah!"

Was it a groan or a call? I gathered my strength for one cry:
"They're coming!" The others heard me and shouted for joy.
What a miraculous apparition! "Schatz . . . it's Schatz!"

Barely two hundred yards away Marcel Schatz, waist-deep
in snow, was coming slowly toward us like a boat on the surface
of the slope. I found this vision of a strong and invincible deliv-
erer inexpressibly moving. I expected everything of him. The

shock was violent and quite shattered me. Death clutched at me and I gave myself up.

When I came to again, the wish to live returned and I experienced a violent revulsion of feeling. All was not lost! As Schatz came nearer, my eyes never left him for a second: twenty yards . . . ten yards . . . he came straight toward me. Why? Without a word he leaned over me, held me close, hugged me, and his warm breath revived me.

I could not make the slightest movement. My heart was overwhelmed by such tremendous feelings, and yet my eyes remained dry.

"It is wonderful—what you have done!"

I was clear-headed and delirious by turns. Schatz looked after me and while the others were shouting with joy, he put his rope around me. The sky was blue—the deep blue of extreme altitude, so dark that one can almost see the stars. We bathed in the warm glow of the sun. Schatz spoke gently:

"We'll be moving along now, Maurice, old man."

I could not help obeying him, and with his assistance succeeded in getting up and standing in balance. He moved on gradually, pulling me after him. I seemed to make contact with the snow by means of two strange stiltlike objects—my legs. I could no longer see the others.

Having walked a couple hundred yards, and skirted around an ice wall, suddenly without any warning we came across a tent. We had bivouacked two-hundred yards from camp. Couzy got up as I appeared, and without speaking embraced me. Terry threw himself down in the tent and took off his boots. His feet, too, were frostbitten. He massaged them and beat them unmercifully.

The will to live stirred in me and again I tried to take in the situation. Our Dr. Oudot could save our feet and hands by the proper treatment. I heartily agreed to Schatz's suggestion that we go down immediately to the lower Camp IV that the Sherpas had reestablished. Terray wanted to remain in the tent, and as he flayed his feet with the energy of desperation he cried out:

"Come and fetch me tomorrow if necessary. I want to be whole. Or dead!"

Rébuffat's feet were affected as well, but he preferred to go down to Oudot immediately. He started the descent with Lachenal and Couzy, while Schatz continued to look after me—for which I was deeply grateful. He took the rope and propelled me gently along the track. The slope suddenly became very steep, and the thin layer of snow adhering to the surface of the ice gave no purchase. I slipped several times, but Schatz, holding me on a tight rope, was able to check me.

Below there was a broad track. No doubt the others had allowed themselves to slide straight down toward the lower Camp IV, but they had started an avalanche that had swept the slope clear of snow. As soon as we drew in sight of the camp the Sherpas came up to meet us. In their eyes I read such kindness and such pity that I began to realize the full measure of my plight. They were busy clearing the tents that the avalanche had covered with snow. Lachanel was in a corner massaging his feet.

I hurried everyone up: We must get down—that was our first objective. As for the equipment, well it could not be helped; we simply must be off the mountain before the next onslaught of the monsoon. For those of us with frostbitten limbs it was a matter of hours. I chose Aila and Sarki to escort Rébuffat, Lachenal and myself. I tried to make the two Sherpas understand that they must watch me very closely and hold me on a short rope. For some unknown reason, neither Lachenal nor Rébuffat wished to rope.

While we started down, Schatz, with Angtharkay and Pansy, went up to fetch Terray, who had remained on the glacier above. Schatz was master of the situation—none of the others were capable of taking the slightest initiative. After a hard struggle, he found Terray.

"You can get ready in a minute," he said.

"I'm beginning to feel my feet again," replied Terray, now more amenable to reason.

Then the descent began. Angtharkay was magnificent, going first and cutting comfortable steps for Terray. Schatz, coming down last, carefully safeguarded the whole party.

Our first group was advancing slowly. The snow was soft and we sank in up to our knees. Lachenal grew worse; he frequently stopped and moaned about his feet. Rébuffat was a few yards behind me.

I was concerned at the abnormal heat, and feared that bad weather would put an end here now to the epic of Annapurna. It is said that mountaineers have a sixth sense that warns them of danger—suddenly I became aware of danger through every pore of my body. There was a feeling in the atmosphere that could not be ignored. Yesterday it had snowed heavily, and the heat was now working on these great masses of snow, which were on the point of sliding off. Nothing in Europe can give any idea of the force of these avalanches. They roll down over a distance of miles and are preceded by a blast that destroys everything in its path.

The glare was so terrific that without glasses it would have been impossible to see. Lachenal was a long way behind us and every time I turned round he was sitting down in the track. He, too, was affected by snow blindness, though not as badly as Terray and Rébuffat, and had difficulty finding his way. Rébuffat went ahead by guesswork, with agony in his face, but he kept on. We crossed the couloir without incident, and I congratulated myself that we had passed the danger zone.

The sun was at its height, the weather brilliant and the colors magnificent. Never had the mountains appeared to me so majestic as in this moment of extreme danger.

All at once a crack appeared in the snow under the feet of the Sherpas, and grew longer and wider. A mad notion flashed into my head—to climb up the slope at speed and reach solid ground. Then I was lifted up by a superhuman force, and as the Sherpas disappeared before my eyes, I went head over heels. My head hit the ice. I could no longer breathe, and a violent blow on my left thigh caused acute pain. I turned round and round like a puppet. In a flash I saw the blinding light of the sun through the snow that was pouring past my eyes. The rope joining me to Sarki and Aila curled round my neck—the Sherpas shooting down the slope beneath would shortly strangle me, and the pain was unbearable. Again and again I crashed into solid ice as I went hurtling from one serac to another, and the snow crushed me down. The rope tightened round my neck and brought me to a stop. Before I had recovered my wits I began to pass water, violently and uncontrollably.

I opened my eyes to find myself hanging head downwards, with the rope round my neck and my left leg in a short hatchway of blue ice. I put out my elbows toward the walls to stop the unbearable pendulum motion that sent me from one side to the other, and caught a glimpse of the final slopes of the couloir beneath me. My breathing steadied, and I blessed the rope that had withstood the strain.

I simply had to try to get myself out. My feet and hands were numb, but I was able to make use of some little nicks in the wall. There was room for at least the edges of my boots. By frenzied, jerky movements I succeeded in freeing my left leg from the rope, and then managed to right myself and to climb up a yard or two. After every move I stopped, convinced that I had come to the end of my strength, and that in a second I should have to let go.

One more desperate effort, and I gained a few inches—I pulled on the rope and felt something give at the other end—no doubt the bodies of the Sherpas. I called, but hardly a whisper issued from my lips. There was a deathlike silence. Where was Gaston?

Conscious of a shadow, as from a passing cloud, I looked up instinctively; two scared black faces were framed against the circle of blue sky. Aila and Sarki! They were safe and sound, and at once set to rescue me. I was incapable of giving them the slightest advice. Aila disappeared, leaving Sarki alone at the edge of the hole; they began to pull on the rope, slowly, so as not to hurt me, and I was hauled up with a power and steadiness that gave me fresh courage. At last I was out. I collapsed on the snow.

The rope had caught over a ridge of ice, and we had been suspended on either side; by good luck the weight of the two Sherpas and my own had balanced. If we had not been checked like this we should have hurtled down another 1,500 feet. There was chaos all around us. Where was Rébuffat? I was mortally anxious, for he was unroped. Looking up I caught sight of him less than a hundred yards away:

"Anything broken?" he called out to me.

I was greatly relieved, but I had no strength to reply. Lying flat, and semiconscious, I gazed at the wreckage about me with unseeing eyes. We had been carried down for about 500 feet. It was not a healthy place to linger in. I instructed the Sherpas:

"Now—Doctor Sahib. Quick, very quick!"

By gestures I tried to make them understand that they must hold me very firmly. In doing this I found that my left arm was practically useless. The elbow had seized up—was it broken? We should see later. Now, we must push on to Oudot.

Rébuffat started down to join us, moving slowly; he had to place his feet by feel alone; he, too, had fallen, and he must have struck something with his jaw, for blood was oozing from the corners of his mouth. Like me, he had lost his glasses and we were forced to shut our eyes. Aila had an old spare pair that did very well for me, and without a second's hesitation Sarki gave his own to Rébuffat.

We had to get down at once. The Sherpas helped me up, and I advanced as best I could, reeling about in the most alarming fashion, as they held me from behind. I skirted round the avalanche to our old track, which started again a little farther on.

We now came to the first wall. How on earth should we get down? I asked the Sherpas to hold me firmly:

"Hold me well because . . . " And I showed them my hands.

"Yes, sir," they replied. I came to the piton; the fixed rope attached to it hung down the wall and I had to hold on to it—there was no other way. My wooden feet kept slipping on the ice wall, and I could not grasp the thin line in my hands. Without letting go I endeavored to wind it round them, but they were swollen and great strips of skin came away and stuck to the rope and the flesh was laid bare. Yet I had to go on down; I could not give up halfway.

"Aila! Pay attention!"

To save my hands I now let the rope slide over my good forearm and lowered myself like this in jerks. On reaching the bottom I fell about three feet, and the rope wrenched my forearm and wrists. The jolt was severe and affected my feet. I heard a queer crack and supposed I must have broken something—no doubt it was the frostbite that prevented me from feeling any pain.

Rébuffat and the Sherpas came down and we proceeded, but it seemed to take an unconscionably long time, and the plateau of Camp II seemed a long way off. Every minute I felt like giving up; and why, anyway, should I go on when for me everything was over? My conscience was quite easy; everyone was safe, and the others would all get down. Far away below I could see the tents. Just one more hour—I gave myself one more hour and then, wherever I was, I would lie down in the snow. I would let myself go, peacefully.

Setting this limit somehow cheered me on. I kept slipping, and on the steep slope the Sherpas could hardly hold me. The track stopped above a drop—the second and bigger of the walls we had equipped with a fixed rope. I tried to make up my mind, but I could not begin to see how I was going to get down. I pulled off the glove I had on one hand, and the red silk scarf that hid the other, which was covered in blood. This time everything was at stake—and my fingers could just look after themselves. I placed Sarki and Aila on the stance from which I had been accustomed to belay them, and where the two of them would be able to take the strain of my rope by standing firmly braced against each other. I tried to take hold of the fixed rope; both my hands were bleeding, but I had no pity to spare for myself. I took the rope between my thumb and forefinger, and started off. At the first move I was faced at once with a painful decision; if I let go, we should fall to the bottom; if I held on, what would remain of my hands? I decided to hold on.

Every inch was a torture I was resolved to ignore. The sight of my hands made me feel sick; the flesh was laid bare and red, and the rope was covered with blood. I tried not to tear the strips right off; other accidents had taught me that one must preserve these bits to hasten the healing process later on. I tried to save my hands by braking with my stomach, my shoulders, and every other possible point of contact. When would this agony come to an end?

I came down to the nose of ice that I myself had cut away with my ax on the ascent. I felt about with my legs—it was all hard. There was no snow beneath. I was not yet down. In panic I called up to the Sherpas:

"Quick! Aila! Sarki!"

They let my rope out more quickly and the friction on the fixed rope increased.

It felt as though all the flesh was being torn off my hands. At last I was aware of something beneath my feet—the ledge. I had made it! I had to go along it now, always held by the rope; only three yards, but they were the trickiest of all. It was over. I collapsed up to my waist in snow, and no longer conscious of time.

When I half-opened my eyes Rébuffat and the Sherpas were beside me, and I could distinctly see black dots moving about near the tents of Camp II. Sarki spoke to me, and pointed out two Sherpas coming up to meet us. They were still a long way off, but all the same it cheered me up.

I had to rouse myself; things were getting worse and worse. The frostbite seemed to be up to my calves and my elbows. Sarki put my glasses on for me again, although the weather had turned gray. He put one glove on as best he could; but my left hand was in such a frightful state that it made him sick to look at, and he tried to hide it in my red scarf.

The fantastic descent continued, and I was sure that every step would be my last. Through the swirling mist I sometimes caught glimpses of the two Sherpas coming up. Snow began to fall, and we now had to make a long traverse over very unsafe ground where it was difficult to safeguard anyone; then, fifty yards farther, we came to the avalanche cone. I recognized Phutharkay and Angdawa mounting rapidly toward us.

I heaved a deep sigh of relief. I felt now as if I had laid down a burden so heavy that I had nearly given way beneath it. Phutharkay was beside me, smiling affectionately. How can anyone call such people "primitive"? The Sherpas rushed toward me, put down their sacks, uncorked their flasks. Ah, just to drink a few mouthfuls! Nothing more. It had all been such a long time.

Phurharkay lowered his eyes to my hands and lifted them again, almost with embarrassment. With infinite sorrow, he whispered: "Poor Bara Sahib—Ah."

Camp II was near. Phutharkay supported me, and Angdawa safeguarded us both. Phutharkay was smaller than I, and I hung on round his neck and leaned on his shoulders, gripping him close. This contact comforted me and his warmth gave me strength. I staggered down with little jerky steps. Summoning what seemed my very last ounce of energy, I begged Phutharkay to give me yet more help. He took my glasses off and I could see better then. Just a few more steps—the very last.

My friends all rallied round. They took off my gloves and my cagoule and settled me into a tent already prepared to receive us. I found this intensely comforting: I appreciated my new existence that, though it would be short-lived, was for the moment so easy and pleasant. In spite of the threatening weather the others were not long in arriving: Rébuffat was first—his toes were frostbitten, which made it difficult for him to walk. He looked ghastly, with a trickle of blood from his lips and signs of suffering writ large on his face. They undressed him and put him in a tent to await treatment.

Lachenal was still a long way off. Blind, exhausted, with his frostbitten feet, how could he manage to follow such a rough and dangerous track? In fact, he got over the little crevasse by letting himself slide down on his bottom. Couzy caught up with him on his way down and, although desperately weary himself, gave him invaluable assistance.

Lionel Terray followed closely behind them, held on a rope by Schatz, who was still in fine fettle. The first man to arrive was Terray, and Marcel Ichac went up toward the great cone to meet him. Terray was blind, and clung to Angtharday as he walked. He had a huge beard and his face was distorted by pain into a dreadful grin. This "strong man," this elemental force of nature who could barely drag himself along, cried out:

"But I'm still all right. If I could see properly, I'd come down by myself."

When Terray reached camp Oudot and Noyelle were aghast. Once so strong, he was now helpless and exhausted.

Immediately after, Schatz and Couzy arrived, and then Lachenal, practically carried by two Sherpas. From a distance it looked as though he was pedaling along in the air, as he threw his legs out in front in a most disordered way. His head lolled backwards and was covered with a bandage. His features were lined with fatigue and spoke of suffering and sacrifice. He could not have gone on for another hour. Like myself, he had set a limit that had helped him to hold on until now. And yet Biscante, at such a moment, still had the spirit to say to Ichac:

"Want to see how a Chamonix guide comes down from the Himalaya?"

Ichac's only reply was to hold out to him piece of sugar soaked in adrenaline.

It was painful to watch Terray groping for the tent six inches from his nose: He held both hands out in front of him feeling for obstacles. He was helped in, and he lay down; then Lachenal, too, was laid on an air mattress.

Everyone was now off the mountain and assembled at Camp II. But in what a state! It was Oudot's turn to take the initiative, and he made a rapid tour of inspection. Faced with the appalling sight that we presented, his countenance reflected, now the consternation of the friend, now the surgeon's impersonal severity.

He examined me first. My limbs were numb up to well beyond the ankles and wrists. My hands were in a frightful condition; there was practically no skin left, and the little that remained was black, and long strips dangled down. My fingers were both swollen and distorted. My feet were scarcely any better; the entire soles were brown and violet, and completely without feeling. The arm that was hurting me did not appear to be seriously injured, and my neck was all right.

I was anxious to have Oudot's first impression.

"What do you think of it all?" I asked him, ready to hear the worst.

"It's pretty serious. You'll probably lose part of your feet and hands. At present I can't say more than that."

"Do you think you'll be able to save something?"

"Yes, I'm sure of it. I'll do all I can."

This was not encouraging, and I was convinced that my feet and hands would have to be amputated.

Oudot took my blood pressure and seemed rather concerned. There was no pressure in the right arm, and the needle oscillated slightly, indicating a restricted flow of blood. After putting a dressing over my eyes to prevent the onset of ophthalmia, he said:

"I'm going to see Lachanel. I'll come back in a moment and give you some injections. I used them during the war and it's the only treatment that's any use with frostbite. See you presently."

Lachanel's condition was slightly less serious. His hands were not affected, and the black discoloration of his feet did not extend beyond the toes. That would probably not prevent him from climbing and from continuing to practice his profession as a guide.

Rébuffat's condition was much less serious. His feet were pink except for two small gray patches on his toes. Ichac massaged him with Dolpyc for two hours and this appeared to relieve him; his eyes were still painful, but only a temporary affliction. Couzy was very weak, and would have to be considered out of action. That was the balance sheet.

As epic as had been his descent from the summit, Herzog's trials were only now starting. Their ghastly retreat off the mountain and back to Kathmandu—both Herzog and Lachanel were carried out on the backs of Sherpas—was no less remarkable and chilling than their ascent, entailing perilous river crossings, torturous injections and almost daily amputations. We rejoin Herzog during his penultimate day in Nepal before the long voyage home.

On July 12, 1950, we left Kathmandu. According to custom, our shoulders were draped with magnificent garlands of sweetly scented flowers. The Maharajah, full of thoughtful attentions, had ensured that my return should be effected as comfortably as possible, and I was borne out on a luxurious litter carried by eight men; the all too familiar jerky movements resumed as we wound up toward the pass.

The path wound up toward the hill and soon lost itself in the jungle. The garland of flowers spread its fragrance around me. I gazed one last time at the mountains in the blue distance, where the great giants of the earth were gathered in all their dazzling beauty.

The others were far ahead. The jolting began anew, bearing me away from what would soon be a land of memories. In the gentle languor into which I sank, I tried to envisage my first contact with the civilized world, of landing at Orly and meeting family and friends. In fact, I could not then imagine the violent emotional shock I would experience nor the sudden nervous depression that would take hold of me. The countless surgical operations in the field—that sickening butchery that shook even the toughest natives—had gradually deadened our souls, and we were no longer able to value the true horror of it all. A toe carved off and tossed away; blood flowing and spurting; the unbearable stench of suppurating wounds—all this left us unmoved.

In the airplane before landing, Lachanel and I would put on fresh bandages for our arrival. But the minute we started down the iron ladder all those generous eyes looking up at us with such pity would at once tear aside the masks behind which we had steeled ourselves for so long. We were not to be pitied, and yet, the tears in those eyes and the expressions of distress would suddenly bring me face to face with reality. Such a strange consolation for my suffering to bring me!

Rocking in my litter, I meditated on our adventure now drawing to a close, and on our unexpected victory. Men often talk of an ideal as a goal toward which one strives but never attains; yet for each of us, Annapurna was an ideal realized. In our youth we had not been misled by fantasies, nor by the bloody battles of modern warfare that pervert the imaginations of the young. For us the mountains formed a natural field of activity where, playing on the frontiers of life and death, we had found the freedom we had sought without knowing it and which was the ultimate need of our nature. The mountains had bestowed on us their beauty and grace, and we adored them with a child's simplicity and revered them with a monk's veneration.

The Annapurna we approached in spiritual poverty is now the treasure on which we live. With this realization, we turn the page: A new life begins.

There are other Annapurnas in the lives of men.

TRAPDOOR

by Admiral Richard E. Byrd

Trapdoor granted with permission from *Alone* by Richard E. Byrd. © Marie A. Byrd 1966, published by Island Press, Washington, DC & Covelo, CA

A dmiral Richard Evelyn Byrd, the great aviator and polar explorer, made many record flights during the pioneering days of Arctic exploration, including the first flights over the North and South poles. In 1933, his expedition was bivouacked at Bolling Advance Weather Base, "planted in the dark immensity of the Ross Ice Barrier, on a line between Little America and the South Pole." It was the first inland station ever occupied in the world's southernmost continent. The original plan was to staff the base with several men; but this proved impossible. In consequence, Byrd had to choose whether to give up the base entirely—and the scientific mission with it—or to man it by himself. Admiral Byrd chose the latter, lured by "one man's desire to be by himself for a while and to taste peace and quiet and solitude long enough to find out how good they really are."

May was a round boulder sinking before a tide. Time sloughed off the last implication of urgency, and the days moved imperceptibly one into the other. The few world news items which Dyer read to me (over the radio) from time to time

seemed as meaningless as they might to a Martian. My world
was insulated against the shocks running through distant
economies. Advance Base was geared to different laws. On getting up in the morning, it was enough for me to say to myself:
Today is the day to change the barograph sheet, or, Today is the
day to fill the stove tank. The night was settling down in earnest.
By May 17th, one month after the sun had sunk below the horizon, the noon twilight was dwindling to a mere chink in the
darkness, lit by a cold reddish glow. Days when the wind brood-
ed in the north or east, the Barrier became a vast stagnant shadow surmounted by swollen clouds, one layer of darkness piled
on top of the other. This was the polar night, the grim aspect of
the Ice Age. Nothing moved; nothing was visible. This was the
soul of inertness. One could almost hear a distant creaking as if
a great weight were settling.

Out of the deepening darkness came the cold. On May 19th,
when I took the usual walk, the temperature was 65 degrees
below zero. For the first time the canvas boots failed to protect
my feet. One heel was nipped and I was forced to return to the
hut and change to reindeer mukluks. I felt miserable; my body
was racked by shooting pains—exactly as if I had been gassed.
Very likely I was; in inspecting the ventilator pipes next morning I discovered that the intake pipe was completely clogged
with rime and that the outlet pipe was two-thirds full. Next
day—Sunday the 20th—was the coldest yet. The minimum thermometer dropped to 72 degrees below zero; the inside thermograph, which always read a bit lower than the instruments in the
shelter, stood at 74 degrees; and the thermograph in the shelter
was stopped dead—the ink, though well laced with glycerin, and
the lubricant were both frozen. So violently did the air in the
fuel tank expand after the stove was lit that oil went shooting all
over the place: To insulate the tank against similar temperature
spreads I wrapped around it the rubber air cushion that by some
lucky error had been included among my gear. In the glow of a
flashlight the vapor rising off the stovepipe and the outlet ventilator looked like the discharge from two steam engines. My fingers agonized over the thermograph and I was hours putting it to

rights. The fuel wouldn't flow from the drums; I had to take one inside and heat it near the stove. All day long I kept two primus stoves burning in the tunnel.

Sunday the 20th also brought a radio schedule; I had the devil's own time trying to meet it. The engine balked for an hour; my fingers were so brittle and frostbitten from tinkering with the carburetor that, when I actually made contact with Little America, I could scarcely work the key. "Ask Haines to come on," was my first request. While Hutcheson searched the tunnels of Little America for the Senior Meteorologist, I chatted briefly with Charlie Murphy. Little America claimed only minus 60 degrees. "But we're moving the brass monkeys below," Charlie advised. "Seventy-one below here now," I said. "You can have it," was the closing comment from the north.

Then Bill Haines's merry voice sounded in the earphone. I explained the difficulty with the thermograph. "Same trouble we've had," Bill said. "It's probably due to frozen oil. I'd suggest you bring the instrument inside, and try soaking it in gasoline, to cut whatever oil traces remain. Then rinse it in ether. As for the ink's freezing, you might try adding more glycerine." Bill was in a jovial mood. "Look at me, Admiral," he boomed. "I never have any trouble with the instruments. The trick is in having an ambitious and docile assistant." I chuckled over that because I knew, from the first expedition, what Fiffe, the Junior Meteorologist, was going through: Bill, with his back to the fire, persuading the yong Fiffe that duty and the opportunity for self-improvement required him to go up into the blizzard to fix a balky trace. That day I rather wished that I, too, had an assistant. He would have taken his turn on the anemometer pole, no mistake.

The frost in the iron cleats went through fur-soled mukluks and froze the balls of my feet. My breath made little explosive sounds on the wind; my lungs, already sore, seemed to shrivel when I breathed.

Seldom had the aurora flamed more brilliantly. And at times the sound of barrier quakes was like that of heavy guns. My tongue was swollen and sore from drinking scalding hot tea, and the tip of my nose ached from frostbite. A big wind, I guessed, would come out of this noiseless cold; it behooved me to look to my roof. I carried gallons of water topside, and poured it around the edges of the shack. It froze almost as soon as it hit. The ice was an armor plating over the packed drift.

At midnight, when I clambered topside for an auroral "ob," a wild sense of suffocation came over me the instant I pushed my shoulders through the trapdoor. My lungs gasped but no air reached them. Bewildered and a little frightened, I slid down the ladder and lunged into the shack. In the warm air the feeling passed as quickly as it had come. Curious but cautious, I made my way up the ladder a second time. Again I lost my breath, but I understood why. A light air was moving down from eastward, and its bitter touch, when I faced into it, was constricting the breathing passages. I turned my face away from it, breathing into my glove, and in that attitude finished the "ob." Before going below, I put a thermometer on the snow, let it lie there awhile and discovered that the temperature at the surface was actually 5 degrees colder than at the level of the instrument shelter, four feet higher. Reading in the sleeping bag afterwards, I froze one finger, although I shifted the book steadily from one hand to the other, slipping the unoccupied hand into the warmth of the bag.

Out of the cold and out of the east came the wind. It came on gradually, as if the weight of the cold were too much to be moved. On the night of the 21st the barometer started down. The night was black as a thunderhead when I made my first trip topside. A tension in the wind, a bulking of a shadows indicated that a new storm center was forming. Next morning, glad of an excuse to stay underground, I worked long and hard on the Escape Tunnel by the light of a red candle standing in snow recess. That day I pushed the emergency exit to a distance of twenty-two feet, the farthest it was ever to go. My stint done, I sat on a box, thinking how beautiful was the red of the candle, how white the rough-hen snow. Soon I noticed an increasing clatter of the anemometer cups. The wind was picking up, so I went topside to double-check that everything was secured.

It is a queer experience to watch a blizzard rise. First comes the wind, rising out of nothingness. Then the Barrier unwrenches itself from quietude and the surface, which just before had seemed as hard and polished as metal, begins to run like a making sea. Sometimes, if the wind strikes hard, the drift comes across the Barrier like a hurrying white cloud, tossed hundreds of feet in the air. Other times the growth is gradual. You notice a slithering movement on all sides. The air fills with tiny scraping and sliding and rustling sounds as the first loose crystals stir. Presently they move as solidly as an incoming tide, creaming over the ankles, surging to the waist, and finally buffeting the throat. I have walked in drift so thick I've not been able to see a foot ahead of me; yet when I glanced up, I could see the stars shining through the thin layer just overhead.

Smoking tendrils were creeping up the anemometer pole when I finished my inspection. I hurriedly made the trapdoor fast, as a sailor might batten down a hatch; and knowing that my ship was well secured, I retired to the cabin to ride out the storm. It could not reach me, hidden deep in the Barrier crust. Nevertheless the sounds came down. The gale bawled in the ventilators, shook the stovepipe until I thought it would be jerked out by the roots, pounded the roof with sledge-hammer blows. I could feel the suction effect through the previous snow. A breeze flickered in the room and the tunnels. The candles wavered and went out. My only light was the feeble storm lantern.

Even so, I didn't have any idea how bad it was until I went aloft for an observation. As I pushed back the trapdoor, the drift met me like a moving wall. It was only a few steps from the ladder to the instrument shelter, but it felt like a mile. The air came at me in snowy rushes; I breasted it as I might a heavy surf. No night had ever seemed so dark. The beam from the flashlight was choked in its throat; I could not see my hand before my face.

My windproof was caked with drift by the time I got below. I had a vague feeling that something had changed while I was gone, but what, I couldn't tell. Presently I noticed that the shack was appreciably colder. Raising the stove lid, I was shocked to find that the fire was out, though the tank was half full. I decided that I must have turned off the valve unconsciously before going aloft; but, when I put a match to the burner, the draught down the pipe blew out the flame. The wind, then, must have killed the fire. I got it going again, and watched it carefully.

The blizzard vaulted to gale force. Above the roar the deep, taut thrumming note of the radio antenna and the anemometer guy wires reminded me of wind in a ship's rigging. The wind direction trace turned scratchy on the sheet; no doubt drift had short-circuited the electric contacts. Realizing that it was hopeless to attempt to try to keep them clear, I let the instrument be. There were other ways of getting the wind direction. I tied a handkerchief to a bamboo pole and ran it through the outlet ventilator; with a flashlight I could tell which way the cloth whipped. I did this at hourly intervals, noting any change of direction on the sheet. But by 2 o'clock in the morning I'd had enough of this periscope sighting. If I expected to sleep and at the same time maintain the continuity of the records, I had no choice but to clean the contact joints.

The wind bellowed. The Barrier shook from the concussions overhead and the noise was as if the world were tearing itself to pieces. I could scarcely heave the trapdoor open. The instant it came clear I was plunged into a blinding smother. I came out crawling, clinging to the handle of the door until I made sure of my bearings. Then I let the door fall shut, not wanting the tunnel filled with drift. To see was impossible. Millions of pellets exploded in my eyes, stinging like BB shot. It was even hard to breathe, as snow instantly clogged my mouth and nostrils. I struggled toward the anemometer pole on hands and knees, scared that I might be bowled off my feet if I stood erect. One false step and I should be lost forever.

I found the pole, but not until my head collided with a cleat. I managed to climb it, too, though ten million ghosts were tearing at me, ramming their thumbs into my eyes. But the errand was useless. Drift as thick as this would foul the contact points as quickly as they were cleared; besides, the wind cups were spinning so fast that I stood a good chance of losing a finger in the process. Coming down the pole, I had a sense of being whirled violently through the air, with no control over my movements.

The trapdoor was completely buried when I found it again after scraping around for some time with my mittens. I pulled at the handle, first with one hand, then with both. It did not give. It's a tight fit, anyway, I mumbled to myself. The drift has probably wedged the corners. Standing astride the hatch, I braced myself and heaved with all my strength. I might just as well have tried hoisting the Barrier.

Panic took me then, I must confess. Reason fled. I clawed at the three-foot square of timber like a madman. I beat on it with my fists, trying to shake the snow loose; when that did no good, I lay flat on my belly and pulled until my hands went weak from cold and weariness. Then I crooked my elbow, put my face down and said over and over: "You damn fool, you damn fool."

Here for weeks I had been defending myself against the danger of being penned inside the shack; instead, I was now locked out. Nothing could be worse, especially since I had only a wool parka and pants under my windproofs. Just two feet below was sanctuary—warmth, food, tools, all the means of survival. All these things were an arm's length away, but I was powerless to reach them.

There is something extravagantly insensate about an Antarctic blizzard at night. It's vindictiveness cannot be measured on an anemometer sheet. It is more than just wind; it is a solid wall of snow moving at gale force, pounding like storm surf. The whole malevolent rush is concentrated upon you as upon a personal enemy. In this indifferent blast of sound you are reduced to a crawling thing on the margin of a disintegrating world. You can't see, can't hear, can hardly move. The lungs gasp after the air is sucked out of them, and the brain is shaken. Nothing in the world will so quickly isolate a man.

Half-frozen, I stabbed toward one of the ventilators, a few feet away. My mittens touched something round and cold. Cupping it in my hands, I pulled myself up. This was the outlet ventilator. Just why, I don't know, but instinct made me kneel and press my face against the opening. Nothing in the room was visible, but a dim patch of light illuminated the floor, and warmth rose up to my face. That steadied me.

Still kneeling, I turned my back to the blizzard and considered my options. I thought of breaking in the windows in the roof, but they lay two feet down in hard crust, and were reinforced with wire besides. If only I had something to dig with, I could break the crust and stamp the windows in with my feet. The pipe cupped between my hands supplied the first inspiration; maybe I could use that to dig with. It, too, was wedged tight; I pulled until my arm ached, without budging it; I had lost all track of time, and the despairing thought came to me that I was lost in a task without an end. Then I remembered the shovel. A week before, after leveling drift from the last light blow, I had stabbed a shovel handle up in the crust somewhere to leeward. But how to find it in the avalanche of the blizzard?

I lay down and stretched out full length. Still holding the pipe, I thrashed around with my feet, but pummeled only empty air. Then I worked back to the hatch. The hard edges at the opening provided another grip, and again I stretched out and kicked. Again no luck. I dared not let go until I had something else familiar to cling to. My foot came up against the other ventilator pipe. I edged back to that, and from the new anchorage repeated the maneuver. This time my ankle struck something hard. When I felt it and recognized the handle, I wanted to caress it.

Embracing this thrice-blessed tool, I inched back to the trapdoor. The handle of the shovel was just small enough to pass under the little wooden bridge which served as a grip. I got both hands on the shovel and tried to wrench the door up; my strength was not enough, however. So I lay down flat on my belly and worked my shoulders under the shovel. Then I heaved, the door sprang open, and I rolled down the shaft. When I tumbled into the light and warmth of the room, I kept thinking, How wonderful, how perfectly wonderful.

SAVAGED BY A LION

by Ben East

Savaged by a Lion from *SURVIVAL 23 True Sportsmen's Adventures*
© Copyright 1967 by Ben East, Published by Outdoor Life Books

The leopard bait was an impala that had been shot and hung in an acacia tree on the edge of a dry river bed. It had ripened in the hot sun for three days, long enough that John Kingsley-Heath and Bud Lindus were sure if there were leopards in the country they could not resist it. The hunting party had hung a number of baits—zebra, gazelle, impala—but for some reason both the hunter and his client felt that this was the one that would get them what they hoped for.

The time was August of 1961. Kingsley-Heath was on safari with the Lindus family—Bud, his wife Pamela and their fourteen-year-old son Roger—along the Ruaha River in the semiarid desert country of central Tanganyika.

Operating out of Nairobi and conducting hunts in Kenya and Tanganyika at the time, John Kingsley-Heath was rated among the top hunters of Africa. He had held a professional hunter's license since 1951, barring a brief interruption during the Mau Mau insurgency, and was known by name and reputation to many sportsmen in the United States.

Lindus was a retired oil salesman from Honolulu and he and his wife were old clients of John's. Bud rated African hunting very high, and Pam and the boy shared his enthusiasm for it.

The chief object of their hunt was a trophy lion. Two years earlier Lindus and Kingsley-Heath had been led up the garden by an enormous maned male, in the Kajiado district of Kenya. That one had the uncanny ability of disappearing at exactly the crucial minute, whether they approached him on foot or by car. He hid in the day, ate their baits at night. Try as he would, Bud never locked his sights on him.

He had come back to Africa now determined to do better. Buffalo and kudu also were on his list. He wanted a good leopard for his wife, and if they came across an elephant with satisfactory ivory they didn't mean to turn it down.

They had sharpened their hunting senses on buffalo in the thick bush country of northern Tanganyika before moving down to the Ruaha. Two bulls had gotten within a yard of them before going down permanently. After that they felt they were ready to take on most anything, including the biggest lion in Tanganyika—if they could find him.

Camp had been made on the bank of the Ruaha, under large acacia trees that spread overhead like huge green umbrellas. Thousands of sand grouse watered in front of the tents every morning. The wing shooting was superb, and they were soon out of shotgun shells and sending back to Nairobi for more.

Alvin Adams, a friend of Bud's from the States, had come out to join them for a fortnight, wanting a big leopard, and was hunting with Kevin Torrens, the second hunter/guide on the safari. The numerous leopard baits had been hung partly in the hope of helping Al get his cat.

Bud and John hunted lions, elephants and kudu for days with no success. Tracks and signs were plentiful but they couldn't come across anything of the sort they desired. Leopards refused to touch their baits, and they began to wonder whether their luck was in or out. But when they hung the impala in the tree at the edge of the river two or three miles from camp, Kingsley-Heath had a hunch they were going to get action.

Three days later, Bud, Pam, Roger and Kingsley-Heath came into camp for a late lunch. When they finished their sandwiches and tea, John suggested they go have a look at the bait. It was time for things to be happening if they were going to.

They drove out in the hunting car, through dry scrub-thorn country, taking along two gunbearers and trackers, Kiebe and Ndaka. Halfway to the leopard bait, however, John sent them off to follow up some elephant tracks, with instructions to rejoin him near the bait tree.

They drove the hunting car to within six hundred yards of the tree, left it and walked carefully the rest of the way. One peep around a large bush told them that a leopard had taken his fill. It was late afternoon, almost time for him to return for his evening meal. There was not a minute to waste. They'd sit for him at once.

It was quickly decided that Pam should have the first chance. Bud and Roger went back to the car to wait; Pam and John stole carefully up behind a thick bush and secreted themselves in the bottom of it, first making a little hole for their guns.

Pam was carrying a rifle of European make, as light as the Tanganyika game laws permitted, for the sake of minimum recoil, mounted with a 4X scope. Kingsley-Heath's gun was a Winchester Model 70 in .300 Magnum caliber, with a 6X Kollmorgen scope. Neither of the rifles was right for what was going to happen, but there were good reasons for choosing them.

Sitting up for a leopard can be sticky business, especially if you are not used to it, since you know that if you fail to make a clean kill you have one of the most dangerous animals in Africa to deal with. Pam was nervous, and said so. Unless the cat fell dead at her shot, she had asked John to back her by putting another into it immediately.

That was why the hunter had brought the scope-sighted Winchester. A 6-power scope may seem unusual for job of that kind, but it has its advantages. To begin with, it enables the hunter to increase his distance from the bait, and often he can select a better hide by moving off a bit. Too, a leopard almost invariably comes on a bait late, when the light is failing fast, and the more powerful the scope the better its light-gathering ability.

Had the two gunbearers not been off following the elephant tracks, Kingsley-Heath would have had one of them in the hide with him, carrying his .470 Westley-Richards double, but he couldn't very well handle two guns by himself.

He and Pam made themselves comfortable, with their rifles trained on the spot where they expected the leopard to appear. For twenty minutes nothing happened. The silence of late afternoon was settling over the bush. Puffs of wind blew through the acacias, stirring up little dust devils, but the breeze was from the bait tree, so they had no worry on that score. Now and then a bird twittered, and the shrunken river whispered around its sandbars. Save for those small sounds, nothing broke the stillness.

It was an uneasy quiet, and as the minutes dragged on John grew suspicious. Was the leopard approaching from behind? Had he scented them and slunk away? They kept a sharp watch all around, nothing stirred in the brush or grass. The time ticked off and John's uneasiness grew. Then, suddenly aware of movement or noise behind his right shoulder, he turned his head ever so slowly and was looking a huge maned lion in the face, just twenty feet away.

The situation was clear to him in a flash. The leopard had not come to the bait because the lion had kept him away. The lion couldn't reach the impala himself, and now, hungry, disappointed and angry, he had spotted the two people in their thick bush, had not seen or smelled enough of them to know what they were, and was stalking them for a kill. And he was close enough for that final, lightning-fast rush with which a lion takes his prey at the last second.

When Kingsley-Heath turned his head and they stared into each other's eyes, the big cat recognized him for a man, but it was too late for that to make any difference. John saw his expression change from the intent look of a stalking lion to one of rage. His face wrinkled in a snarl and he bunched his feet under him for the spring.

It all happened a great deal quicker than it can be told. One second John was staring at the leopard bait. The next he was looking the lion in the face, the animal was gathering for its leap, and the hunter was swiveling his rifle around from the hip.

"The eyes of the big cats, I think more than those of any other animal, mirror what is going on behind them," Kingsley-Heath told me long afterward. "At the instant of attack those of a lion seem to be on fire. The burning yellow orbs of this big male fairly blazed into mine, and there was no misreading his message."

John did not wait to bring the rifle to his shoulder. He was sitting on his hunkers, as he described it, and he whipped the gun across his knees and pulled off at the lion, all in a split second, trying for the thickness of the shoulder. The shot struck a little too far back, but the animal reacted to the 180-grain soft-nose as most lions do to a hit, whipping his great head around and biting savagely at the wound.

Pam and John were not conscious, then or afterward, of running through the six-foot bush where they were hidden, but they did it and never got scratched. They got clear and raced for the car. In the thicket behind them simba was growling and roaring and thrashing in pain and anger. They ran until they were far enough away to be safe, then stopped to get their breath and congratulate themselves on a very narrow escape.

"We have to get this chap," John told Bud when they finished panting out their story. "You and I will have a lion war."

The two gunbearers were not yet back from their elephant scout. Pam and Roger were left in the car, and Lindus and Kingsley-Heath took their heavy rifles and hurried off. John's was the .470, Bud's a .450/400 double made by Manton & Co., a London firm. Both were good lion guns, but because they had not expected to encounter a lion and had thought they might get a chance at an elephant that afternoon instead, they had only solid ammunition along instead of the softnose loads they would have preferred.

The lion had left the place where he was shot, and it was plain from the blood that he was reasonably well hit. The blood spoor led down to the bottom of the dry river bed. There, although he was bleeding heavily, it had dried in the sand and lost its color, making it difficult to follow in the evening light.

He ran along for a ways under the bank, climbed up a small gully and went into the thicket of mswaki bush, and evergreen that grows like very thick weeping willow, with the outer branches draping down to the ground, leaving a cave-like opening underneath. This thicket was leafy, the lion had left little signs on the hard-baked sand, and the two men went down on their hands and knees to track him though gaps between the bushes.

They didn't crawl far before Kingsley-Heath pulled up short. "This is no good," he told Bud. "If we go ahead with our eyes on the ground we'll walk right down his throat. Kiebe and Ndaka should be back at the car by now. We'll get them and let them do the tracking while we watch over their heads."

Kiebe was a particularly good man to have along in such a situation. A Kamba by tribe, he had hunted for twenty-five years, eight of them with John, and before that with Miles Turner, one of the most famous of East African white hunters. John had saved Kiebe's life a time or two, and the tracker had saved his. Tracking down a wounded lion was nothing new to Kiebe, and he was absolutely fearless. Kingsley-Heath knew he could count on him no matter what happened. The second tracker, Ndaka, was a stand-in, but willing and brave.

The two of them were at the car, and the four hurried back to the place where John and Lindus had left the lion track. It was lucky they had quit when they did, for fifteen yards ahead they found the bloodstained bed where he had been lying.

He had moved about thirty yards into another thicket while they were gone, still bleeding. They tracked him foot by foot, with Kiebe in the lead. It was not a job any of them liked, but they had no choice. Once a hunter starts an affair of that kind it's up to him to finish it, no matter how sticky it gets.

Kiebe wiped warm blood off the leaves, and held up a hand to warn his bwana that they were getting close. Then the lion announced his presence with an angry growl from the mswaki just ahead, and they saw him race across a narrow opening into the next brush.

It was almost dark now and in a very few minutes they'd have to give up. They left the track and circled, hoping to push him into the open, but nothing stirred and no sound came from the thicket. They wasted precious time, the light got worse, and at last John whispered to Kiebe in Swahili, "This is for tomorrow. We'll let him stiffen up and beat him out in the morning."

The tracker's reply was a finger jabbed sharply to the left. There, under a low bush fifty feet away, the lion lay broadside, breathing heavily, watching them. John could barely make out the shape of his heavy body in the dusk.

The range was close enough, but they were shooting with open sights in very bad light and had to be absolutely certain of a hit. Kingsley-Heath took Lindus by the arm without saying a word, and they shortened the distance to forty feet, moving warily to the nearest tree, where a leaning branch would give them a rest for the rifles.

The shot belonged to the client, and since Bud was a first-class rifleman John did not expect there'd be any need for him to fire. But he made one serious mistake. He overlooked the fact that in the half-darkness the flash of Bud's rifle would blind him for the critical fraction of a second when the lion might come for them in case Bud failed to kill it where it lay.

Bud's 400-grain solid took the cat in the shoulder a bit high, but because the bullet was not a softnose it went all the way through without opening up, doing only slight damage to the lungs. And in that instant when John should have hammered another in, he could see neither lion, thicket nor anything else.

In all the years he had been a professional hunter, and all the hunting he had done on his own, Kingsley-Heath had been attacked by an animal only once. That had happened in the very beginning, when he was training under an old hunter. He approached too close to an elephant he was stalking, and the bull knew he was there. It waited until he was within reach, grabbed him up in its trunk and sent him flying into a swamp tangle. By good fortune he escaped unhurt except for a slight stiffness in the right shoulder. This time he wasn't going to be that lucky.

The lion came in a rush the first few feet, then covered the rest of the distance in two great bounds. John had time only to yell at Bud to dodge behind him, when a huge ball of snarling fury landed at his feet.

He slammed a 500-grain solid into the great cat's head between the eyes, point blank, and but for a fluke that would have ended the affair. But because the lion was badly wounded, when he hit the ground in front of John his head jerked forward and down, like a man who has jumped off a stool. The heavy bullet struck him square between the eyes, as the hole in the skull showed later, but instead of going through his brain and leaving him deader than mutton, it passed down between his lower jaw bones and out at the side of his throat, hardly more than blinding him with the rifle flash.

He leaped past John within a foot and landed between the two men, headed for Bud. John saw that Bud's rifle was tangled in branches and he couldn't get it down. The quarters were too close for a second shot without endangering him. Kingsley-Heath took one step and clubbed the lion on the head with the barrels of his .470 as hard as he could. The cat grunted, shook his head and wheeled around, and before John had time to pull the second barrel he pounced.

A quarter ton of growling, raging cat hit Kingsley-Heath full length and he went down as if he had been electrocuted. It felt about like that, too, he said afterward. There was no pain and he was not stunned, but the shock of the blow as the lion crashed into him, with its forepaws over his shoulders and its huge body bearing him to the ground, was beyond description. His gun went flying out of his hands and then he was lying on his back with the lion on top of him, its front legs wrapped around him and its paws under his shoulder blades.

A lion, even wounded, often pauses for a second after his initial leap has knocked his victim down, and this one did just that. That tiny pause saved John Kingsley-Heath's life. He knew that within a second or two the lion would bite him through the head, and he smashed his right fist into its nose with every ounce of strength he had. He broke the bones of the hand, but the lion opened its mouth at the punch, maybe to growl, and John followed through. He rammed his fist down its throat, and its teeth closed on his arm halfway to the elbow.

John heard the bones crunch, but in a strange detached way, not as a sound from outside, but as if he were hearing the arm break from inside his own body.

So long as he kept his fist down its gullet, the lion could not get at his head or throat. He could feel its claws under him, ripping his sheepskin hunting jacket to shreds and his back with it. He knew that if it got its hind feet in his belly it would tear his guts out with one rake. He twisted on his left side, drew his legs up to protect himself, and concentrated on trying to keep his broken arm in its mouth.

The statement has been made more than once that a man attacked by one of the big carnivores is overcome with a merciful numbness, so that he feels little or no pain or fright at the time, perhaps because shock overwhelms his nervous system. Kingsley-Heath thinks the part about being benumbed is true, but for a different reason. The victim of such an attack is fighting for his life and knows it, and he believes that a man in that situation has little sense of feeling. In his own case he felt very little pain through the whole mauling. When it was all over his back looked as if he had been flogged with a cat-o-nine tails, but it hadn't hurt while it was happening.

Nor did he smell the lion's breath or have any sensation of feeling its mane against his face, although he knew it was there. He did have a bad nightmare in the hospital later, when he felt lion saliva all over his fingers and woke up in a cold sweat trying to get his mangled arm out of the cat's jaws.

Actually the lion took care of that for him. It shook him as a terrier shakes a rat, rolling him back and forth, and freed itself of his fist and arm about the way a big fish gets rid of a bait.

It takes far longer to describe such an experience than to live through it. Everything was happening at once. "Get my gun!" John yelled at Kiebe in Swahili. "Kamata bunduki yanga! Piga the bloody thing!" Piga means hit, but in this case he meant shoot and the tracker knew it.

Then he saw Bud come into sight over the lion's rear quarters and the .450 bellowed twice. But because John was lying under the cat Bud could only shoot far back. They learned later that he broke a hind leg but the lion paid no attention, neither flinching nor turning its head. It just went on growling and mauling its victim, and took no notice of Bud, Kiebe or Ndaka. That is typical lion behavior. Once simba gets his victim down he stays with it. A wounded leopard will rush from one member of a party to another, biting at the first man he can reach, then striking instantly at a fresh victim, only to leave that one and run for the next. A lion takes time to finish what he begins.

Kiebe grabbed up Kingsley-Heath's gun now, checked swiftly to see which barrel was loaded, ran in and shoved the muzzle against the lion's shoulder, heedless of his own danger. But from where John lay beneath the brute he saw that the bullet, whatever it might do to the cat, would also smash through his knees, and he screamed at Kiebe, "For God's sake don't shoot there!"

The tracker backed away a step and blasted the one round remaining in the .470 into the lion's back just behind the shoulders. That put Kiebe out of the fight, for the rest of John's ammunition was in his pocket under the lion. But the shot was strong medicine and well placed. It broke the spine, and the beast twisted off him. A wounded lion doesn't quit as long as he is breathing, however, and this one wasn't finished yet. Back it came on its front legs, with its back end dragging, and quick as John moved he wasn't quick enough to get to his feet before it was on him again.

It would have taken him through the left side of the chest with its huge canine teeth, and one bite there meant certain death, but he threw up his left arm to fend it off. He had not time to jam the arm down its throat, as he had done with the right. He simply shoved it into the lion's face. It grabbed and crushed the arm just above the wrist, and once more John heard his own bones break like match sticks, not as he would have heard another man's but as a noise coming from inside him.

At this point Ndaka did a very brave thing. He threw himself on the lion and stabbed it again and again in the ribs and throat with a 6-inch knife. Then Lindus, who had been stuffing fresh shells into the breech of his double while Kiebe got in his shot, stepped close and sent two more solids crashing into the lion. The great body jerked and sagged and rolled off Kingsley-Heath.

As he struggled to his knees, half helpless from two broken arms, he jabbed his left foot into its face to kick it himself away. That was the wrong thing to do, even with a lion breathing its last. Its jaws closed on John's shoe and it bit down, and for the third time he heard the crunch of breaking bones, in his foot and ankle now. And that time, he remembered, it hurt like hell! He wrenched his foot free, but the lion died with his shoe in its mouth.

They left the cat where he lay. They'd have to run the risk of hyenas tearing him up before morning. Bud and the natives carried John to the car and wrapped him in the rain curtains to keep him warm. Then they set off in the darkness for camp. There was no moon and they couldn't follow their tire tracks, so rather than get lost they stopped and made a fire, and let off a shot every ten minutes. It's a rule on safari that if anyone fails to return to camp by an hour after dark the search and rescue operation gets under way at once. They knew that by now Kevin Torrens, the other white hunter, was out looking for them.

Kingsley-Heath's wounds had clotted well and he was bleeding only a little, but he drank water like a mad thing. Kiebe and Ndaka left to try to find the way to camp, and shortly after that the injured hunter and his clients heard the hum of a motor, and then the lights of Kevin's Landrover appeared.

It was 2 o'clock in the morning by the time they found their way back through the scrub thorn to camp. Torrens cleaned up John's wounds, poured disinfectant into them, and had him swallow three times the normal dose of antibiotic tablets, washing them down with hot tea. Next John got down two cups of soup and began to feel quite comfortable. But about that time he went into shock, started to tremble violently from head to foot and kept it up for hours.

They had a radio telephone in camp, but by now it was Sunday morning (the lion attack had occurred on Saturday evening) and the government radio in Nairobi was closed down, so Torrens left for the nearest phone at Dodoma, a hundred and twenty miles away, thirty of it rough track through the bush, to call for a plane. They had scratched out a small airstrip near camp earlier.

Kevin got through to Peter Whitehead, a manger of a leading Nairobi safari firm, at 6:15 on Sunday morning and forty-five minutes later Dr. Brian McShane, Kingsley-Heath's physician and good friend, was airborne and on the way with a supply of blood and the other things he needed to fix the injured man up temporarily. Bill Ryan, another professional hunter from Nairobi and also an old friend of John's, came along to take over the safari. It was a two-and-a-half-hour flight. They touched down at the camp at 9:30 that morning.

By that time John had sent the safari boys out and they had brought the lion to camp. The hyenas had not molested it, after all. It was a magnificent brute, the biggest Kingsley-Heath had ever had a hand in killing: 10-1/2 feet long and weighing out at 497 pounds. It must have weighed a bit above 500 alive, before it lost blood. There in the Dodoma district the lions live mostly on buffalo and the full-grown males are among the finest trophies in all of Africa. This one was paler than average, but not quite a blond, with a lavish mane. As his friends remarked later, at least John had been savaged by a decent lion, not one with just a ruff around its neck. Bud got the pelt, and it's a safe bet he will never take a trophy that will give him a more exciting time. John kept a tooth and claw and had them mounted as paper-weights.

Dr. McShane poured blood into him and set about patching him up for the flight back to Nairobi. He had two broken arms, a broken hand, a foot chewed and badly crushed, a horribly lacer-ated back and a few deep holes in various parts of his body. As he was being carried into his tent after the attack, he had heard Kiebe tell the other safari boys, "Bwana ameliwas na simba," which is Swahili for, the bwana was eaten by a lion.
Kingsley-Heath entered the Princess Elizabeth hospital in Nairobi that afternoon, August 13, and stayed until October 2. He was on the dangerous list for a few days, but the surgeons repaired his broken bones and, by great good fortune, he escaped infection, which is very likely to follow an attack by one of the big cats because of their habit of feeding on putrid meat. The fact that he had been able to get down a massive dose of antibiotics a few hours after the accident probably saved his life. He did not think that the lion was cleaner than average.

The mauling proved far worse than the aftermath, and most of his stay in the hospital was not a bad ordeal. Bud and Pam finished their hunt as they had planned, with Bill Ryan's help. They took a couple of fine kudu, and by the time they got back to Nairobi two weeks later John was able to sit up and drink champagne with them, by way of celebrating his escape. He was well enough to leave on an easy safari the day he got out of the hospital.

For the courage he had shown, Kiebe received the Queen's Commendation for Brave Conduct a few months later. Asked what his thoughts were at the time, he replied matter-of-factly, "Do you suppose I am going to do nothing when a lion is about to kill my friend?" And the only reward he wanted was corrugat-ed iron to roof his house.

There was an interesting sequel to the story. On August 12, 1962, a year to the day from the time the lion mauled him, he sat up for leopard at that same tree and at the same hour. He had a lady client again, and they sat in the same bush where Pam and he had waited. The leopard put in an appearance as the light was starting to fade, the client fired and the cat tumbled, hit hard but not dead. In the twinkling of an eye John found himself in exactly the same predicament he had faced on that fateful evening a year earlier, except that this time he was dealing with a leopard rather than a lion. Not that that is much to be preferred.

It was too dark for tracking, so they went back to camp and returned the next morning. The blood spoor led into a bush nearby, and to the hunter's great relief the leopard lay dead there. So if there was any jinx connected with that tree it had been laid to rest. But in all of Africa there is not another tree that John Kingsley-Heath will remember so vividly and long as that acacia on the edge of the dry river bed. He says so himself.

In 1821, Sir John Richardson (Surgeon/Naturalist for Franklin) undertook his expedition to the Canadian arctic under the aegis of the British Geographical Society. However, as so often happens, once disaster struck, science became a secondary concern to survival.

ARCTIC ORDEAL

by Sir John Richardson

Arctic Ordeal from *The Journal of John Richardson*, Surgeon-Naturalist with Franklin, 1820-1822;
Edited by C. Stuart Houston.

With permission of McGill-Queen's University Press

FRIDAY SEPTEMBER 14TH, 1821

The officers being assembled round a small fire of willows this morning, before starting, Pierrot [Pierre St Germain] presented each of us with a small piece of meat that he had saved from his allowance. It was received with great thankfulness and such an act of self denial and kindness, being totally unexpected in a Canadian, filled our eyes with tears. The lake appearing to terminate, at the distance of a few miles, in a river we directed our course thither, and during our march we met Credit who communicated the joyful intelligence of his having killed two deer in the morning. We instantly halted and having shared the deer that was nearest to us, prepared breakfast.

After breakfast the other deer was sent for and we went down to the river [Burnside River], which was about 200 yards wide, and flowed with great velocity through a broken rocky channel. The canoe being put into the water, an attempt was made to cross at the head of a rapid, where the current was rather smoother than elsewhere. Mr. Franklin, Pierez and

Belanger embarked first, but they proved too great a load for the canoe, particularly as there was a fresh breeze blowing at the time, which rendered it more difficult to manage. In consequence, conjoined with the unskillfulness of Belanger, who was unaccustomed to a small canoe, they got involved in the rapid and upset in the middle of it. They kept hold of the canoe, however, until they touched a rock where the water did not reach higher than their middles. Notwithstanding the strength of the current, they kept their footing, here, until Pierez, with great dexterity, emptied the water out of the canoe, replaced Mr. Franklin in it, and finally embarked himself. Belanger was left standing in a very perilous situation on the rock, but the other two were also in considerable hazard, for the canoe had been much damaged and actually sank before the traverse was completed. This time however it was in shallower water; they reached a small rocky island and having again emptied out the water re-embarked and reached the other side in safety. In the meantime Belanger was suffering extremely, immersed to his middle in a strong current where temperature was very little above the freezing point, and the upper part of his body covered with wet clothes and exposed to a strong breeze not much above zero. He called piteously for relief and Pierez on his return endeavored to embark him, but in vain. Pierez himself now was rendered incapable of further exertion by the cold, but having brought the canoe to the shore, Adam attempted to embark Belanger but found it impossible, from his situation in the middle of the rapid, and there was a deep channel betwixt him and either shore. An attempt was next made to carry out a line to him made of the slings of the mens loads. This also failed, the current acting so strongly upon it, as to prevent the canoe from steering, and it was finally broken and carried down the stream. At length when Belanger's strength seemed well nigh exhausted, the canoe reached him, with a small cord belonging to one of the nets and he was dragged perfectly senseless through the rapid. He was instantly stripped and being rolled up in blankets, two men undressed themselves and went to bed with him — but it was some hours before he recovered his warmth and sensation.

By this disastrous accident Mr. Franklin's portfolio, containing his journal, and astronomical and meteorological observations, was carried down the stream and lost. The most of the party and almost all the baggage were transported across in the course of the afternoon although the canoe filled with water at every traverse.

Pierre St Germain, the interpreter, was presumably a native of the Northwest, and not a French-Canadian voyageur. He was the most successful hunter by far, occasionally helped by Adam, the other interpreter, and by Augustus and Junius, the two Eskimos. Credit was the only voyageur who had much success in hunting: Credit shot a caribou on 31 July and again on 26 August, a muskox on 29 August 1821, and two caribou on 14 September.

Margaret Crotty may have graduated with honors from college, but it was her summers past working as a lifeguard that saved her life the following January (1996). The following epic commenced twelve miles off the coast of Northern Sumatra, one of the largest islands in the vast (17,000 islands) Indonesian archipelago.

LOST AT SEA

by Margaret Crotty as told to Jan Goodwin

I was swimming in the deep waters of the Andaman Sea, just north of Sumatra. It was nighttime, and the sea looked black. Constantly buffeted by the icy waves, I could no longer kick with my left leg, which was beginning to throb. When I reached down, I realized my ankle was deeply gouged. I kept trying to lift my leg to see how bad the wound was, and when I finally did, I could see that it was bleeding freely.

Now I was truly afraid. This region teemed with sharks. What if the blood attracted them to me?

An hour before I was sitting on the crowded deck of the ferry Gurita, en route from northern Sumatra, one of the largest of Indonesia's 17,000 islands, to the outlying island of Weh. I was happily contemplating the weekend ahead, with thoughts of collapsing with a good book on one of Weh's fabulous beaches. Shortly after graduating from college in 1994, I'd moved to Indonesia, and for the last six months had been interning with the Jakarta office of the international relief and community development organization "Save the Children." After working in the field for two weeks—I'd been living in a tiny village with hardly any running water, electricity or modern conveniences—I was ready for a few days of relaxation.

The other passengers had the same idea: It was Friday, January 19, 1996, the weekend before Ramadan, the Muslim month of fasting. People were traveling home to their families, and the mood was festive; one lovely elderly lady insisted that I share her cake. We were almost two hours into the two-and-a-half-hour journey, about six miles from our destination, when we felt the ferry's first sickening lurch.

It's extraordinary how quickly things happen. Later, a government investigation found that the 25-year-old Gurita had been navigating through rough seas with six-foot waves, carrying nearly double her passenger capacity, plus a heavy load of cement. So when she sprang a few leaks (the investigators never figured out why), the ferry started sinking alarmingly fast, first listing one way, then the other, all the while throwing screaming passengers from side to side.

The holiday atmosphere turned to panic and chaos. The Gurita suddenly tipped over on her side. No alarm was sounded, but it was clear that we had to abandon ship. Terrified, some people threw themselves into the sea.

Everyone else seemed too hysterical or frozen in fear to think of grabbing a life preserver, so I ran to a locker and started handing them out to the crowd. Even though Indonesians are islanders, few know how to swim. This is particularly true of women: Indonesia is the largest Muslim nation in the world, and swimming for women is considered immodest.

Fortunately, I knew how—and knew well, having been a lifeguard as a teenager. So when the life preservers ran out, I didn't panic. It didn't occur to me that I might need one myself. On some level, I assumed that rescue would be imminent. I had no idea that I'd be spending the next 16 hours swimming for my life.

The boat lurched again, and suddenly I found myself falling inside the life-preserver locker. The heavy lid slammed shut; I was trapped inside. As the ferry tipped over on its side, water started rushing in. I thrashed trying to get out, but no go. The locker was soon completely submerged, and I was swallowing enormous amounts of water. Everything began to take on this yellow glow; I was browning-out. This is it, I thought. This is what it's like to die.

I must have been underwater for almost three minutes when I finally managed to kick the locker door open, which is probably how I gouged my left ankle. I groped my way through the enclosed part of the deck, where the locker was, and suddenly popped out in the open. I broke the surface, gasping for air, absolutely exuberant and astonished to be alive. I'd had a brush with death, and now I was saved.

THE DEATH RAFT

On the surface, I couldn't see very much. It was about 8:30 p.m., and cloudy, so there was no moonlight. Some waves parted, and I spotted the life raft nearby. Five feet away, a man struggled to keep afloat. Swimming over to him, I pulled him to the raft. With perhaps 50 people on it, the raft was very crowded, but the only raft around that I could see. Everyone had swarmed to it. Some were trying to grab onto flotsam—small benches, suitcases, lockers—but when those things sank, they'd make their way over to the raft.

But it was filling up fast, and everyone on it was panicking. Over the waves, I could hear pockets of people praying: "Allahu Akbar" ("God the Greatest"), over and over. Their chanting would calm them down; then, as it grew in intensity, it would make them frantic again. At that moment, praying struck me as folly. Instead, I grabbed the rope that went around the raft and hung on.

That's when I noticed that there were very few women and no children on the raft. I guess that was because the men had been out on the open deck when the ferry went down, so they could get off earlier, while most of the women were below and hampered by their children and babies.

More people started climbing up on the life raft. Finally, inevitably, one compartment popped and quickly deflated; another sprang a leak. Its hissing was a terrible sound. A man near me said, "As soon as the raft goes, you've got to move away, because people will drag you down."

As the raft collapsed, I started to swim away. But I couldn't get far. A terrified European man, maybe 35, attached himself to me. "Stefan," as I'll call him, must have been in shock: He kept hanging on to me as if I were a life preserver—sometimes even pulling me under. A compartment of the raft was still floating, so I tried to bring him back to it. But he kept clutching me.

To keep both of us afloat, I knew I needed some help. I remembered from a rescue and water-safety course that you could create a flotation device by tying the ankles of your pants, blowing into them, then holding onto or tying off the waist, which is what I did with my drawstring pants. It made a bubble about the size of my head. I held it with one hand, and swam with the other. It wasn't very buoyant, but it provided some hope.

When people saw I could float, they started paddling toward me. There was one woman who kept coming at me. Each time she approached, I would have to leave Stefan, then take her back to what was left of the raft. She'd always return. I couldn't hold on to both, and I didn't know what else to do. I wasn't thinking clearly, rather I was numb, just responding to whatever was happening. Over and over, an extremely frightened Stefan would ask me if we would survive. I kept saying we would. One time, after taking the woman back to the remains of the raft, I turned around and saw that Stefan was no longer there. He'd slipped under. Desperate, I started to look for him. Then I saw his body bobbing in the water. It was terrible to realize he'd drowned. Minutes went by, and when I turned to look for the woman, she was gone as well.

SWIMMING WITH SHARKS

I felt sick with sadness and guilt, as though I'd failed them. It was about then that I checked my throbbing ankle, and realized I was bleeding heavily in shark-infested waters.

Awash in fear, alone in the dark, I was sure I could see shark fins—every wave crest looked like one. I knew I could swim and tread water, but there was nothing I could do if sharks came at me. I desperately tried to concentrate, to remember what I knew about sharks, any information I could recall from watching the Discovery Channel or reading National Geographic. Would they surround me, would there be just one? Is there any way to fend them off?

It was just as well that, at the time, I didn't know what a local newspaper reported several days later: Three sharks had been caught in the area. In their stomachs were parts of humans that they'd fed off of, as well as bits of clothing—even shoes.

Why was I spared? Partly timing. As I learned later from an expert, during the night the sharks native to this particular region tend to feed close to the shoreline, and I had unwittingly made my way to deeper waters. But I have no idea nor any theories on what saved me the following morning. Most likely, I was just plain lucky.

THE NIGHT WATCH

Hours went by. I knew I mustn't panic, or I would surely drown. I kept telling myself, "Margaret, you know you can swim, you know how to float." I kept thinking about how lucky I was to have such great friends to go home to, how supportive my parents and two brothers and sister have always been, and how horrible they'd feel if I didn't make it. I was only 23, and there were so many things I wanted to do. I also thought about Stefan and how his fear had forced me to stay calm. I felt grateful to him: By reassuring him, I had helped myself.

Where the Andaman Sea joins the Indian Ocean, the currents are swift and powerful. Throughout the night, I was being carried farther and farther away from the wreckage. At one point, I spotted a small light in the distance, which I later learned was a lighthouse. I tried to swim toward it, but I kept getting pulled away in different directions.

The converging currents also caused the waves to crash in on one another, creating whirlpools in which I kept getting caught. Wreckage from the ferry, from metal railings to broken wood parts, swirled around and bashed into me. Swimming couldn't get me out of these traps; the currents were too strong. But I discovered that if I dove under them, I could escape for a time.

Coping with the whirlpools and the strong currents was sapping my energy. I was becoming very tired. My mouth was raw from swallowing so much salt water. I kept looking for anything I could hold onto. Several times, I reached out in the dark for what I thought was floating debris. Each time, I touched a human corpse. I told myself, over and over, "If you can last until dawn, someone will see you, and you will be rescued."

As dawn began to break, the waves became much higher. I longed to rest and tried to float, but the swells were enormous and swamped me from many directions. Resting was impossible. Every minute was a fight to stay above water. Even though I was now miles away from where the ferry sunk, travel bags, plastic sandals, pocketbooks and other such tokens of the accident continued to float past me. It was chilling to think that yesterday these things had belonged to living, celebrating people. Now where were they?

My one source of comfort was my watch. Amazingly, it was still working—I could tell by its glow during the night. Somehow, it made me feel a tiny bit more in control. If it could keep going, I felt, then I could, too.

I'd been in the water 14 hours when an Indonesian man wearing a life jacket and lying on a large ferry cushion appeared. I called to him; he replied, "I can't help you—I can't swim." I said, "I know. I'm just so glad to see somebody else." He said he was glad to see me, too. His name was Jauhari; I called him "Joe" for short. He had cookies and some lollipops, and he gave me one. It was the first food I'd had, and the sugar gave me a lift.

Suddenly, in the far distance, I saw a small plane and a helicopter that looked like they could be part of a rescue search. I got so excited, I ripped off my T-shirt—which I had wrapped around my injured ankle to check the blood flow—and began waving it in the air. I yelled to Jauhari—who was being swept away on top of the currents—to look at the sky. But they went away, no doubt having failed to spot us.

THE NAKED SKY

I was despondent and, by now, very sunburned. I'm a redhead, and my back and face were blistering. My mouth and eyes were swollen from the salt water. I was nearing exhaustion, physically and emotionally. But I kept talking to myself: "You can't give up now, not after all you've been through."

Being miles from where the ferry sank meant I was a long way from the search area. At dawn, I'd hoped to see fishing boats, but there were none. I passed what seemed like island after island, but the currents were so strong, I always got swept away before I could reach shore. Eventually, they carried me to the tip of the northwesternmost island of the Indonesian archipelago. I knew, from maps I'd seen before, that if I missed this island, and if the currents continued to carry me along in the same direction, the next land mass would be Sri Lanka, nearly a thousand miles away.

THE LAST ISLAND

It was at this point—the 15-hour mark—that I realized my situation was do or die: Either I swim to this island—struggling against the current in my state of exhaustion—or drift indefinitely. It's amazing what you can do when choices like these become clear. I suddenly kicked into high gear and started swimming as hard as I could. To keep up my energy, I kept reminding myself out loud that I'd been swimming since I was four, and that I had been challenged by my grandmother to swim one and a half miles across a lake when I was 11. Reminding myself of that lesson in endurance gave me strength.

Unfortunately, the pep talks were no help in the steering department: I could see that I was going to hit where there was a sheer rock wall. And sure enough, I was repeatedly smacked against the cutting rocks. My hands were so stiff I could no longer control my fingers; I was so weak, I couldn't grab a handhold. There was nothing to hold onto, anyway, and I kept getting washed back out. Finally, after what felt like endless smashing, one big wave pushed me into a small crevice about halfway up a 15-foot cliff. I got washed out once, but the second time I managed to stay put.

Directly above me, the rocky incline didn't seem so steep. Very slowly, I began to pull myself up. I reached out one arm, rested, then reached out with the other. In this manner, I was able to climb onto a rock, where I fell asleep for a few minutes. But then the sun scorching my back woke me up, propelling me to move. I slowly climbed to the next rock. It took me two hours to travel 10 to 15 feet. My goal was to find a little bit of shade, a tiny rock overhang where I could shelter my head. The sun and heat were intense: I was very close to the equator, and it was 2:30 p.m., the hottest time of day. I was dehydrated, badly burned from my 16 hours in the sea, and by now wearing only my underwear. I'd lost my pants balloon and T-shirt sometime before, and had left my sandals on the ferry. In my mind, there was nothing to do but to walk across the island to the lighthouse that I'd spotted from a distance. At least, I hoped it was on this island—but I wasn't sure. I estimated that it would take about two days to get there. I could eat leaves, I thought, and use them for cover from the sun, and maybe find water. I was delirious to even contemplate such a plan, because by this time I was so weak, there was no way that I'd have been able to accomplish any part of it. My feet were very swollen; I was covered in bruises, scrapes and cuts. The island was rugged and steep and showed no sign of life.

At about 3:30 p.m., while I was resting on a rock, two tiny wooden boats powered by small outboard motors suddenly appeared in the ocean below me. Maybe I'd been spotted by the plane after all? But then, unbelievably, the boats went away. I learned later that the men couldn't turn off their motors and come ashore because the waves would have smashed them to pieces against the rocks. A few minutes later, they returned, hanging back from the rocky shoreline and waving at me to climb down into the water. I was terrified—I couldn't imagine going back into those waves, but I knew I had to do it. I half-climbed, half-slipped back into the water. A man threw a big plastic bottle on a rope, which I grabbed. Then he pulled me into one of the boats.

Shivering with fever, wracked with pain, I collapsed in the bottom of the boat, where they covered me with a jacket and a sarong. I heard one of the men say over a walkie-talkie, "We've got the little American."

SAVED!

We finally made it back to Sabang, my original destination, later that night. On the way, I was carried onto another island — where the head of the village brought me coffee, fed me dates and treated my wounds. During the few hours that I was there, I stopped a rescuer and, thinking of the man who gave me that lollipop, asked, "Did you find Joe?" The man next to him turned around and said, "I'm Joe." I felt relieved that he'd been saved, too.

In Sabang, there was an ambulance and a stretcher waiting for me; I was taken to the local clinic. When we landed, the entire town was waiting on the dock for the news of survivors. Many had photographs of family members who'd been on the Gurita. They showed me the pictures and asked if I'd seen this person or that person; one group was searching for a family of nine. I had to tell them I hadn't. Despite their fear and grief, people reached out to me, saying, "It's the will of Allah that you survived." Looking at them as they waited to hear news of their loved ones, I realized just how lucky I was.

At the hospital, they stitched up gashes in both ankles. I was told that the current had taken me some 30 miles from where the ferry had sunk. In the women's ward, where I spent the night, there were only two passengers, both foreigners: myself and a British woman. One Indonesian woman had survived, but she wasn't in the ward. The men's ward was full of survivors. I couldn't help wondering: Would more women be alive if they'd been allowed to learn how to swim?

By the time the search for ferry passengers was finally called off, 14 days later, police investigators had found only 39 survivors—and were able to recover only 55 bodies out of 338 people who had perished.

At first I didn't want to call my family in New York City and upset them, but the American consulate was issuing a press release. So I talked to my mom and dad, and a few days later my father flew in. When I told my parents I wanted to stay until I finished my work at Save the Children, they understood and didn't pressure me to return.

I couldn't work for a while, though. When I went to see a doctor a few days later in Jakarta, he discovered I had lost so much blood that I was very anemic. I also needed antibiotics because the gouge on my left ankle wouldn't heal. Not only was I sick, but for the first couple of weeks after my rescue, I was depressed and weepy, which I understand is normal enough given the epic I'd just survived.

Only now, seven months after the Gurita went down, is the terrible sadness beginning to fade. Next month, I start as an assistant principal of St. Mark the Evangelist, a grammar school in Harlem, in New York City. I've always wanted to work with underprivileged kids, and I feel lucky to have the chance. I feel lucky to be alive, and lucky that I was brought up in a family where girls were dared to swim cross the lake. Mostly, though, I feel lucky to have survived.

Jaguars are renown for stealth and ferocity, and when wounded, are considered the most savage cats on earth. Such was the scenario facing Sasha Siemel in the Brazilian frontier, circa 1940. In this classic account, the line separating the hunter and the hunted dissolves in an unforgettable drama of life and death.

DEATH IN SILENT PLACES

by Alexander "Sasha" Siemel

During the years that he had been on his crusade of slaughter, Assassino had earned the reputation as a "devil-cat," much the same status successful man-eaters in Africa and Asia are awarded. No bullet could harm him, the thinking went, nor could any man kill him. Anybody who hunted him lost all his dogs and never got so much as a glimpse of his anthracite and amber hide. After killing an estimated 400 head of cattle to the south of the Xarayes, for some reason he became inactive for several months before resurfacing near the Fazenda Descalvados, a large ranch in the Xarayes Pantanal. It may have been that he was injured in a territorial battle or was sick for a while; no one knows.

Alexander "Sasha" Siemel refused to hunt Assassino, although begged to do so by ranchers on several occasions. He was only too aware, as a professional, that to try to hunt the big tigre with his hounds would be a death sentence for them, skilled though they were. And now, without his lead dog

Valente, who might have stood some chance, there was no hope for it. But this decision was made before Assassino killed Jose Ramos.

It was Ramos himself who had ridden into Siemel's camp near Ilha do Cara Cara, his horse lathered and his clothes crusty with sweat. Not taking time to dismount, he implored Siemel to come with his dogs to hunt Assassino, who had killed twelve of his small herd.

Siemel turned him down flat. He would as soon send the fox terrier pup as his jaguar dogs for all the chance they would have. Jose Ramos, desperate, begged again, but the most Siemel could promise was that he would go after the cat if he saw him or knew he was close by. With resignation, Ramos swore to go after Assassino himself. He would kill or be killed. Little did he realize.

Within two day's of Ramos' visit, Siemel noticed a tall, dense column of vultures circling over the marshes some miles off. Suspecting one of Assassino's calling cards, he investigated and soon found the mangled body of a marsh deer, the carcass badly ripped by claws and teeth but the meat uneaten. Incredibly, as he went on with the dogs in close control, five marsh deer in all were found executed by the assassin cat, the spoor of his huge pug marks unmistakable. Not one ounce of meat had been eaten from any of the bodies except by the urubi. Assassino was back in top form.

At the fifth kill, Ravioso lost control and ran off on the scent of the jaguar, Siemel quickly collaring the other dogs lest they take up the deadly trail as well. Clenching his teeth,

Siemel listened to the bass bawling of the lead dog through the long grass, knowing what he would hear soon. It came as a piercing canine scream of agony that stopped abruptly as a slammed door. Assassino had won again.

Siemel was at a loss as to how to hunt this insane tigre through the dense cover of the marshes. Back at camp, having buried the tattered remains of Ravioso, he thought back over the jaguar's career, realizing the apparent impossibility of trying to run down the big cat without dogs, at the same time knowing

that to expose his pack was as good as shooting them. For hours
he pondered the problem. His rifle would be useless in the heavy
grass; only the spear could draw the life blood of the tigre at
such suicidally close quarters. But, he thought, even with the
loss of Raivoso, possibly he could use the dogs to get close
enough to the jaguar to deal with it. He was still wrestling with
the problem the next morning when the thud of Maria Ramos'
horse galloping into camp set little Tupi into a paroxysm of
barking.

Maria was a wreck. Half-hysterical and bush-torn, she
poured out all she knew; that Jose had gone after Assassino and
only the claw-torn horse had returned with blood on the saddle.
To the junglewise tigrero, it was like reading a newspaper head-
line. There was nothing to do but go now and try to find whatever might be left of Jose Ramos. Siemel took four leashed dogs,
two new ones called Amigo and Leon joining with Vinte and
Pardo, and tied the fox terrier to one of the hut poles so he
would not follow. Maria led the way along the river to the place
where she said Jose had cut off the trail, refusing when Siemel
tried to get her to ride home. She was a woman of the pantanal
and insisted on coming.

A mile ahead, the green capao stood like a beacon over
the ocean of grass, a strange, verdant projection like a lichen-
covered rock in a tropical sea. Far above, speck-like vultures
volplaned and circled.

Jose Ramos lay as Assassino had left him, a mass of torn
meat lying on its face. As Siemel rolled the corpse over in a loud
whine of flies, Maria fainted and fell from her horse. She did not
now argue when sent back to the ranch.

The sign was clear: Deep scars marked the spot from which
the jaguar had leaped, and blackening speckles of blood freckled
the grass stems around the hoof marks. Some yards away lay the
unfired percussion gun. Siemel looked around him. If Assassino
had knocked a man from his horse once, he would do it again.
Also, there was no way to spear-fight effectively from horse-
back. Dismounting, he tied the animal to a tree in a small clearing
and unsheathed his zagaya blade. A pistol—the ubiquitous

Smith and Wesson .38 Special revolver, the Brazilian standard against which all other handguns were judged—was in his belt holster. Years later, while spear-fighting a jaguar, Siemel would manage to shoot himself in the leg with this very pistol. In any case, the .38 Special cartridge is of little value against a charging jaguar and was carried for delivering the coup de grace—the brain shot. On a hunch, he also took his bow and two arrows, in case he had the opportunity of provoking a charge with them.

A very simple plan—Siemel decided that the cat was probably still quite close, and, by releasing the dogs and running after them at speed, there was a possibility that he might throw the jaguar's ambush tactics off. Yes, if he could keep up, maybe there was a chance. He let slip the dogs.

After ten minutes of running through the marsh grass, the vocal bedlam of the dogs ever farther ahead, he knew that he had been wrong. The death shriek of Padro, the leader, sounded over the plain and was followed in less than a minute by the screech of the disemboweled Vinte. Within 450 yards, Assassino killed all four dogs in his classic ambush pattern. His lungs on fire, Siemel was sick with fury at finding the last one, Leon, in an opening in the capao. And then another bark filtered through the bush and caught his ear. It was the fox terrier, Tupi, who had chewed through his tether and followed his master's scent.

As the little dog ran by, barking insanely at the cat smell, Siemel slammed his heel over the trailing end of the broken tether, flipping Tupi over as the line tautened in a full run. As the pet yelped in surprise, that same moment there was a rustle of heavy movement just across the clearing. Then ominous silence. Carefully, Siemel laid his spear at his feet and notched an arrow. Without a glance down, he stepped on the little dog's foot, making it shriek with startled pain.

It worked. Across the opening a few stalks of grass twitched. In a single fluid movement, Siemel came to full draw, and his arrow hissed blindly into the tangle as Tupi began to bark again. The thug! of the arrow told Siemel he had touched the jaguar, and there was a flurry of movement through the curtain of grass. Scant seconds ticked by in time with his heaving chest as he sighted his last shaft and sent it whipping into the cover. Would the confusion of the barking dog and the flash of the arrows bring the charge he needed? The answer appeared in a blur of streaking motion as Assassino, a broken-off shaft protruding form the bunched muscles of his shoulder, ran for a low scrub tree out of pure instinct. He was nearly there when he saw Siemel.

The man gulped involuntarily when he saw the jaguar's tremendous size as the cat stopped and then stood glowering at Siemel across a thirty-yard open space. The zagaya in position, the spearman realized that he would never again have a fight like this one, very possibly because he would not be alive for the next one. He had none of the advantages of the dogs to break the concentration of the jaguar, to keep him off balance. Furious with pain in his shoulder, the monster cat would be completely unpredictable in his next attack. The killer cat measured the man, stalking back and forth with guttural growls as if caged, punctuated with screaming roars that fluttered Siemel's guts. Every sense locked on the cat, Siemel began to move slowly in, edging closer, pushing for the charge. Both man and jaguar were searching for an opening. The cat's came first.

It was just the airy flutter of wings, the flap of an urubi vulture settling into a tree above him. But it was enough. The terrible strain broke Siemel's all-important concentration, and he committed the fatal sin of glancing away from the jaguar. In a microsecond, it saw its chance and launched itself straight at the spearman. Off balance, Siemel lunged and pivoted at the same time, the foot-long forged-steel spearhead catching Assassino a lucky slice on the neck as the mottled mass of golden-sheathed muscle hurtled by. A giant, talon-studded paw glanced off Siemel's right shoulder, knocking him down like a flung doll. In that moment he should have been a dead man.

Somehow, probably because of the shock of the neck wound, the cat was also thrown off balance. Siemel gained the second he needed to roll to the side and scramble to his knees, the spearblade once more leveled and weaving for a thrust. As lithe as any cat, Siemel regained his feet. He could feel his strength flowing away like sweat, but Assassino was also showing some effect of the heavily bleeding neck wound. Mere feet between them, the two fighters stood panting, eyes locked, for what seemed to Siemel an eternity. He knew that if he could drive the blade home once more, he would win. The question was really whether he could stand up to the charge that would make that thrust possible. He did not have long to ponder the question. As if reading his mind, through the blue eyes, the jaguar gave a last terrific roar and exploded straight at Siemel.

It was so fast and from so close range that Siemel nearly did not manage to lift the spear point in time. As the irresistible impact slammed through the thick shaft of louro wood, he saw that the blade had caught the throat too high, and a thrill of horror raced over him; so close were the raking claws that he was sure he had held the shaft too far forward. As he had seen Joaquin Guato do, he pushed forward hard, withdrawing the spear, and in the same motion plunged it deep into the chest. With the last of his draining strength, he pinned the jaguar down, the cutting steel buried near the heart. Assassino fought madly, its lashing claws deeply lacerating the spear shaft, scoring the wood as Siemel drove his full weight down. As the tip of the blade passed completely through the chest and grated against the ground on the far side despite the flesh-buried cross-stop, the paw strokes slowed and, with a great shudder, stopped. How long he leaned on the zagaya shaft, Sasha Siemel did not know. He didn't know that Assassino was dead, and he was alive.

Blow-by-blow re-creations of adventure epics are so difficult to pull off that most authors opt for a journalistic reporting style. However, when the blow-by-blow style is used, and when it works, it puts the reader directly into the experience and the immediacy is felt. The following account took place Deep in Canada's northwestern wilderness, a region as unforgiving as a missed paddle stroke on an icy river.

A DEATH ON THE BARRENS

by George James Grinnell

George James Grinnell, *A Death in the Barrens* - a true story, published in 1996 by Northern Books, [Box 211, Station P. Toronto, ON, M5S 2S7, phone/fax - 416-531-8873]. Copyright 1996 by George James Grinnell. Reproduced by permission of Northern Books. Prior to publication, in 1995, this true story was presented by George Grinnell at the 10th Annual Wilderness Canoe Symposium in Toronto.

THE LAST SUPPER

"Just a little ripple," Joe said, his eyes staring into space. He was lying naked on my air mattress with my blanket on top of him. I was also naked astraddle him, rubbing him down.

"Just A Little Ripple!" he repeated louder. The muscles in his neck tensed and the veins stood out like crimped hoses. His whole body began to thrash about.

"Just a little ripple!" he wailed.

I could no longer hold him down. Our one surviving tent was in danger of being destroyed by his wild and uncontrollable movements. The others were waiting outside for Joe to recover his sanity. Art lay dead on the tundra, frozen. Bruce and Skip shivered in the darkness. They were perilously close to freezing also. Peter was trying to cook up some cornmeal in a tin can. The pots, pans, utensils, rifles, fishing gear and all the food that had been in the grey and green canoes had been lost in the rapids.

"George, Pete, help!" Joe cried out.

"You're O.K. now, Joe," I said.

Every muscle in his body was struggling with death. His flailing arms bounced off me, as if he was unaware of my presence. I tried to restrain his tormented body from accidentally tearing down the tent.

"GEORGE, PETE. HELP!" he repeated.

Finally, exhausted from his struggle, Joe fell back onto the air mattress, breathing heavily. I replaced my blanket over him, straddled him once again and continued to rub him down.

"...and then we had breakfast..."

Joe began recalling the events of the day, his eyes staring blankly through the tent walls. "We stopped for lunch..."

"Yes..., yes..., we stopped for lunch," I echoed back to him.

"And then Pete caught a fish..."

"Yes. Yes, and Pete caught a fish..."

"And then we ate lunch..."

"Yes. And then we ate lunch."

"And then we continued down the river..." Joe's eyes began to move about quickly and seemed to almost bulge out of his head. His torso began to thrash about again..

"Just a little ripple!" he said, and propped himself up on his elbows.

"You're all right now, Joe," I said.

"JUST A LITTLE RIPPLE!" he screamed. Every muscle in his body tensed; he began to twist and turn again in agony. "JUST A LITTLE RIPPLE!"

"You're safe now, Joe."

"George, Pete—Help!" he called again, completely oblivious of my presence.

For about an hour, Joe tried without success to work himself back into reality. Darkness was settling over the tundra, and the others were waiting out in the cold while his frantic agonies threatened to tear down our one tent, without which we were sure gonners.

Joe reviewed the events of the day with ever more detail, always returning to that "little ripple"—which had turned out to be a series of treacherous cascades down which we all had been swept. When the succeeding events flooded his consciousness, his eyes stared out in terror, and he began again to flail his arms, his body thrashing about.

September 14th: This has been the most harrowing day of my life [Joe wrote later]. It started as many others recently; bleak and dismal under a cover of clouds. It was below freezing, and the sand was crunchy and hard from its layer of frost and ice.

Once on the river, the pleasant sandy esker country dropped rapidly behind us. We paddled along, no one saying much. Finally, we pulled into a gravelly bay for lunch. George, Bruce and I scurried around looking for wood scraps. Art heated a kettle and Skip and Pete fished from the shore. Almost immediately, Pete latched onto a 17-pound orange-fleshed lake trout and wrestled with him for 20 minutes.

After a fine lunch of fish chowder, we shoved off again at around 2:30. The weather was still dismal, although the wind had dropped. In a few minutes we heard and saw rapids on the horizon.

At the top, the rapids looked as though they would be easy going, a few small waves, rocks. Nothing serious. We didn't even haul over to shore to have a look, as we usually did. The river was straight and we could see both the top and foot of the rough water quite clearly—or thought we could. We barreled happily along. We bounced over a couple of fair-sized waves and took in a couple of splashes, but didn't mind, as I had made an apron of my poncho and remained dry enough. I was looking a few feet in front of the canoe for submerged rocks when suddenly Art shouted, "Paddle."

I took up the beat, at the same time looking farther ahead to see what it was we were trying to avoid. I was surprised to see two lines of white. I looked at them in helpless fascination. It was too late to pull to shore. Our only hope was to pick what appeared the least turbulent spots and head for them. I was not really frightened, but had, rather, an empty, sinking, "It's-all-over-now," feeling. We went over the falls and plunged directly into a four foot wave. The bow sliced in, and a sheet of foaming green engulfed me. The canoe yawed, slowed. The current caught the canoe once again and plunged it toward the next falls a few hundred feet away. By some miracle, Art straightened the canoe out a little, but we were still slightly broadside as we went over the second falls.

This time the bow didn't come up. I could feel the canoe begin to roll over under me. In a few seconds water was all around me, foam and clutching currents pulling me along with the canoe, which by this time had rolled bottom up. The lathered roar stopped, the current lessened. Art and I were clinging to the canoe.

The seriousness of our position had not yet fully dawned on us. At first the water didn't feel uncomfortable. My heavy parka was full of air in between its layers, and I was quite buoyant. Art draped himself over the stern of the canoe and yelled to me to do the same at the bow. Then I saw Bruce and Skip were in the water too, their canoe also having swamped.

The next thing I knew, George and Pete were paddling furiously by us in the red canoe, heading for shore. I watched them as they leaped out, dumped their packs and headed back toward us. Packs were floating all around us. Art was holding onto the canoe with one arm and my pack and his 86-pound camera box with the other. I saw Art's pack floating off in another direction and swam a few yards after it, but by this time my parka was soaked, so I came back to the canoe. I told Art in a dry, disinterested voice that we had just pulled a damned-fool stunt and that this would likely be the end for us. He assured me through chattering teeth that this was not the case and that, although it would be hard, we would pull through in good shape.

George and Pete went after our packs first. To our horror, as George struggled to haul my soaked pack into the canoe, he lost his balance and toppled overboard. George almost overturned the canoe trying to haul himself out of the water. That would have put all six of us in the water. None of us could have got out. Finally Pete paddled to shore, dragging George along. They dumped the water out and came back. This time they managed to drag Bruce and Skip to a small rocky island and leave them there.

By now I was paralyzed by the cold water. I couldn't swim. I couldn't move. Bruce and Skip on the island began shouting, "Hurry up."

[Joe's remembrance of events at this point becomes inaccurate. Skip and Bruce were not yelling "Hit me! Hit me!" to one another. It was Joe who was yelling "Hurry up."]

After lunch, Pete and I followed Art and Joe down the river and over the falls. Like Joe, I had had that sinking "It's-all-over-now" feeling as the bow shot over the first falls and I had a glimpse of what lay below, before being knocked into a daze by that wall of green water at the foot of the first cascade. It hit me so hard I thought I was motionless while the bank zipped by me like an express train going in the wrong direction. Suddenly a second black ledge rose from the bottom of the river towards the canoe. I was jolted back to reality. I dug my blade deep into the fast moving water and feared that the handle would break. With all my strength, I propelled the canoe over the brink at full speed.

"Keep Paddling! Keep Paddling!" I yelled to Peter as the bow plunged.

Before the standing wave hit me, I braced knees under the gunwales of each side of the canoe, and raised the paddle over my head. As we crashed through the wave, I brought the paddle down and pulled with all my strength. The bow came up. Water rolled through the canoe. I turned quickly and saw it roll out the stern behind Peter. I took another stroke as the water rolled back towards the next ledge. With gunwales awash, we sped over the third cascade and through the rapids below. We passed Art and Joe, clinging to their overturned canoe, then crossed the basin to the nearest dry land, unloaded, and emptied the water.

Peter and I hurried back to rescue the others; but on the way, we came across Bruce's pack. I grabbed the leather straps, leaned the canoe down to the water and, using the gunwale as a fulcrum, threw my weight back and flipped the pack aboard. It was a dangerous maneuver.

The next pack we came to was Joe's; it was bigger and heavier than the others and had been floating in the water for a longer time than Bruce's. I tried the same method, but my fingers were swollen and had long since lost feeling. The ice on the leather straps was slippery. I leaned the canoe down once again to the water, used the gunwale as a fulcrum, and threw my weight back to flip the pack aboard; but my numb fingers slipped off the ice-coated straps. Joe's pack returned to the water; I fell against the opposite gunwale. Grasping at a thwart to prevent myself from falling overboard, I saw water flooding over the gunwale into the canoe. Before the canoe tipped over, I kicked backward and somersaulted over the gunwales into the water. Peter fell to his knees, grabbed both gunwales and stabilized the canoe; but it was now once again full of water.

Five of us were now immersed in the freezing water, with only moments to live. Two of the canoes were floating upside down; the third was full of water; the provisions upon which we depended for our survival had either sunk in the rapids or were floating temporarily in the basin, or were being carried downstream by the current; and the lives of every member of the expedition depended on Peter Franck.

As I clung to the side of our canoe, Peter urged me to swim. There was an island in the basin not far away but our progress was very slow. The sleeve of my jacket, soon soaked, became too heavy to lift. I kicked until I lost feeling in my legs; soon they were dragging uselessly, weighted down by my heavy Army boots. I held onto the bow with my left arm and tried to swim on my back with all my remaining strength, but our progress was painfully slow.

I decided I would have to remove my clothes if I were to be of any help to Peter, which was a mistake. When I unzipped my jacket, the icy water flooded around my chest, cramped my muscles and sucked the wind out of my guts. I couldn't breathe. Desperately, I tried to pull my chest out of the water; and, once again, I nearly tipped the canoe over. I looked at Peter and saw terror in his face; he fell to his knees and tried to stabilize the canoe. Climbing aboard was out of the question. I fell back and tried to swim again, until my arm became so tired I could not lift my arms out of the water. Thinking myself finished, I let go of the canoe to enable Peter to reach the island. My heavy Army boots dragged me down, and the icy water closed over my head.

Looking death in the face, I fought my way back to the surface, recovered my grip on the gunwale, and once again tried to swim while the icy water swirled through my open jacket and drained the remaining strength from my body.

"Keep Swimming. Just keep Swimming," Peter urged. I looked up at him. He was so close, and yet so far away. His eyes were out on stilts. He was not looking at me, but staring at something ahead. I turned and saw the island moving away from us. The canoe was in current. We were being swept past the island downstream to a certain death. With my last remaining strength, I redoubled my efforts; but my legs were useless, my right arm nearly so, and the sleeve of my jacket too heavy to lift. There was no hope. Peter's only chance of survival depended on me letting go of the canoe. Once again I sank to the bottom, but this time not nearly so far.

"I can Touch. I can Touch." I yelled joyfully, my head just emerging from the water. I held the canoe against the force of the current, and Peter worked the canoe towards the island. As my body came out of the water, I tried to walk; but with no feeling in my legs, I had to crawl instead.

After emptying the canoe, Peter helped me back in. He handed me my paddle. I had no feeling in my hands. I dropped it. He picked it up and handed it to me again. I dropped it again. The third time, I stared at my fingers and gripped the paddle with all my strength. I could no longer feel where my hands were, but I could still see them. I told them what to do as if I were operating a robot.

I threw my shoulders forward and watched my arms, dangling like leather straps, follow. When the blade struck the water, I pulled. The canoe surged forward once again.

The more I paddled, the more I recovered, and soon I was a help to Peter; but icy wind continued to blow through my open jacket, cooling my skin and drawing the warmth, and life, out of me.

At first, Peter headed towards the grey canoe, with Art hanging onto its stern and Joe onto the bow. The grey canoe had been the first to capsize. Art and Joe had been in the water the longest, but before we reached them, we heard other voices calling: "George, Pete, Help!" Words that Joe would repeat over and over again in his approaching delirium.

We abandoned Art and Joe and turned to rescue Skip and Bruce first. They were clinging to their overturned green canoe as it was being swept out of the basin downstream.

"George, Pete, Help!" Skip and Bruce cried again. We raced to catch them before they were swept away.

As we came alongside, I yelled at them to hold onto the stern of our canoe behind Peter, and we would drag them to a second island further downstream. Skip held onto the overturned green canoe as well as to ours, and we ran with the current down to the island, where they crawled out onto dry land.

"Hit me! Hit me!" Skip yelled.

"Hit me! Hit me!" Bruce yelled back. They stood facing one another. Water dripped off Bruce's parka and Skip's yellow slicker. They had difficulty making their arms move. They twisted their shoulders; their arms followed, and soon they were able to bring some feeling back to their arms.

"Hit me! Hit me!" they continued to chant.

Peter turned our canoe upstream, and we dug our paddles into the fast water to rescue Art and Joe. Our paddle handles bent, but our progress was slow against the current, and I was nearing total exhaustion.

"Hurry up, hurry up," I heard Joe yell in his husky voice through chattering teeth. Neither he nor Art had called out before, not even when we had turned away from them to rescue Skip and Bruce. Their heavy parkas had protected them from the icy water at first, but now I heard Joe's voice yelling more desperately as the cold sunk into his bones. Ice water against the skin draws off body heat about eighty times faster than air; it can kill a man in about twenty minutes. Their time had nearly run out, and they were only partly conscious.

By the time Peter and I brought our canoe alongside, Art and Joe could only stare up at us with blank eyes. We instructed them, as we had instructed Skip and Bruce, to hold onto our canoe at the stern behind Peter.

Art let go of the overturned grey canoe and held onto our gunwale, but his other hand still gripped tightly his heavy pine camera chest, which held nine thousand feet of film and all his camera equipment. This chest was the means by which he hoped to feed his family; and of this hope he would not let go, even as death came upon him.

Joe grabbed onto our canoe at the stern next to Art, but he would not let go of the over-turned grey canoe. Peter and I strained every muscle, but our progress was slow.

"Let go of the grey canoe!" Peter urged Joe.

My mind became fogged. [Joe wrote later.] I remember Pete shouting to me to grab hold of his canoe. [Pete was shouting at him to let go of the grey canoe.] I did. So did Art. I was holding onto Art's pack. [He had let go of Art's pack and was holding onto both canoes.]

We got nowhere, although George and Pete paddled like fiends. I lost my grip on Pete's gunwale and shouted for him to come back or I would drown. He quickly stopped paddling. I grabbed onto the red canoe again.

The next thing I remember, my feet were scraping over the rocks near the shore. I took one or two steps using every single remaining ounce of strength I had, then collapsed unconscious on the rock and moss shore.

Totally exhausted, I fell out of the bow seat and crawled onto the island alongside Art and Joe. None of us could walk. I lay beside them.

Peter urged me to get back into the canoe to pick up Bruce and Skip downstream. I said I couldn't, and he left without me. Joe lay on the tundra. Art knelt on the gravel and fumbled with the zipper of his Moosehide jacket, trying to get his clothes off: but he had lost all feeling and coordination in his fingers. "What do you want me to do?" He asked.

There was one pack on the island, Bruce's pack. It had been the first pack Peter and I had rescued before my unsuccessful attempt to haul Joe's oversized pack aboard. Peter had left it on the island after dumping the water out of the canoe when we had arrived at this island the first time. I crawled over to it, pulled down on the leather straps to release the buckles, and hauled out Bruce's sleeping bag. I dragged it over to Art and together we tried to get our clothes off. I was slightly more successful than Art. The zipper on my jacket was already undone, but I lacked the coordination to undo the buttons on my shirt.

"What do you want me to do?" Art repeated, while fumbling unsuccessfully with the zipper on his Moosehide jacket.

"Get undressed, and get in this sleeping bag with me," I repeated.

Unable to undo the buttons on my shirt, I thrust my fingers through the opening, clenched my fists, threw back my shoulders and ripped every button off. The icy wind sliced into my wet long johns.

"What do you want me to do?" Art repeated helplessly a third time.

"Get undressed and get into this sleeping bag with me," I answered ritualistically; but my consciousness was now focused almost entirely on my own survival. I ceased to be aware of Art or of anything else, except the cold wind slicing into my wet long johns and drawing the heat of life from my body. I thought of only one thing: Escape. I crawled into Bruce's sleeping bag.

Contrary to popular opinion, freezing to death is not a pleasant way to die. It is so painful, in fact, that I desperately wanted to pass out, to go crazy or (failing that) to die as quickly as possible. During waves of consciousness, my mind raced over the possibilities of making a fire, finding food, or of rescue. I had thought about the Royal Canadian Air Force miraculously landing on the basin, or a band of Innuit hunters stumbling unexpectedly upon us. The chance of this happening was so clearly remote that I soon despaired of survival, and only desired to get rid of the pain as quickly as possible.

I did my best to escape reality, by one means or another; but that was not as easy as it sounds. I was like an insomniac trying to sleep: The pleasant dreams would not come until I had sincerely accepted the inevitability of death. Then they came, but they did not stay. They were so pleasant that they revived my will to live. When first I regained consciousness, the cold, instead of being painful, was ecstatically pleasurable. It reminded me that I had not yet died. Where there is life, there is hope; and my mind raced once again over the possibilities of rescue. Then the hope faded and turned to despair; the pleasure turned to pain; my only desire was to die as quickly as possible, and then the dreams came again.

In the first dream, I had been walking through the woods of New Hampshire on a pleasant Autumn day with the sun pouring down upon me through the orange and red leaves of the maple trees. My second dream was of sitting by a fire in Zaidee's apartment.

Between dreams, before the despair set in once again, I had time to reflect. I reflected on the meaning of death. I tried to visualize my obituary in the paper: "George James Grinnel, age 22, died September 14th, 1995 on a damned fool expedition to the Arctic."

I thought about God. Did I believe that God would save me? I had more faith in a rescue attempt by the Royal Canadian Air Force, and my faith in that was about as minimal as it gets.

I asked myself if I was glad to have come on the expedition. I was very glad. I preferred to die in that lovely Garden of Eden, rather than to have lived my life out in the other world from which I had at last escaped. Better death in the wilderness than life in civilization; yet when I passed out, it was of civilization that I dreamed.

In my third dream, I was lying in bed as a child of about five, and my mother was bringing food up to me. She was calling out, "George, George, are you all right." A strange thought, since my mother had always called me "Jim."

Skip and Bruce had recovered enough to help Peter paddle the red canoe back upstream. They had taken time to pick up a bag of emergency driftwood along the way and to secure Art's pack still floating in the basin. By the time they returned to the island Art, Joe and I were on, the three of us were unconscious.

They undressed Art and put him in the sleeping bag. Peter, the only man who had not fallen in the water, was also, ironically, the only man who carried his matches in a waterproof container. He lit a small fire with our emergency driftwood. He helped Skip move Art near it, and attempted to give Art artificial respiration. Then they removed Joe's clothing, all except his wet long johns, and carried him over to where I was having pleasant dreams.

"George, George, are you all right?" I heard in my dream.

Suddenly I awoke and remembered that I had left Art and Joe out in the cold.

"Yes, I'm fine," I answered; but when I realized my selfishness, I longed to escape once again into that other, more pleasant, dream world. The cold was difficult enough to deal with, but facing my betrayal of Art and Joe was overwhelming.

Joe's foot kicked me in the face.

"We are putting Joe in with you," Skip said.

Joe's delirious, kicking and thrashing body reminded me that he was in far worse pain than I was; I began rubbing him down.

My next recollection [Joe continues], hazy as it is, is one of being in a sleeping bag, with George giving me a brisk rubdown. He kept asking, "How are you feeling, Joe?" and I kept telling him that I was doing fine and to quit pounding on me. I remember that I felt warm and comfortable all over except for my feet, which felt like blocks of ice.

Outside, I could hear Pete and Skip talking in a worried fashion about Art. They had rescued his pack and emergency sack of driftwood; they had undressed him and put him in his sleeping bag by the little fire that Peter had built. They tried to bring him around, but he had not responded, and neither knew what to try next.

After a while, I crawled out of the sleeping bag Joe and I had shared, and asked Skip if he wanted me to get in with Art and try to rub him down. Skip was distraught and grateful for my offer to help. He was still fully dressed in his wet clothing. His yellow water-proof slicker provided some protection against the wind; but his teeth were chattering, and he kept moving about so as not to freeze.

Before I climbed in with Art, I asked him to help me pull my wet underwear off. Naked, I at last felt warm, though the temperature of the air was well below freezing and the wind bitterly cold.

Art's naked body was frozen to the touch and seemed very frail. The side next to the fire was warmer than the other side. After a few minutes, I began to wonder if he was being warmed by the fire or being cooked. Eventually, I had to face the fact that he was dead. I lingered with him for a little longer, my naked body trying to pass some warmth to his naked body; but he lay very still.

Skip and Pete set up the one surviving tent, removed Joe's long johns and placed his tormented body on my air mattress with my blanket on top of him, which he repeatedly kicked off in his struggles. There being little more that could be done, Bruce returned to his sleeping bag, so as not to add another unconscious body in the growing darkness.

Skip was nearing the end of his strength. I emerged from Art's sleeping bag and asked him if he wanted me to go in with Joe to rub him down. He readily agreed, and so I sat astraddle Joe, naked body to naked body, and rubbed his chest.

Every time Joe recalled the events of the day, he would come to that "little ripple" and go raving mad, his arms flailing about uncontrollably, his eyes wide with terror, until, as darkness spread over the tundra, I feared he would tear our one tent down; but finally he tried a different tack and began to recall backwards the events of the day.

"We had lunch..., and before that, Pete caught a fish..."
He seemed calmer. He was staring up at the tent ridge, concentrating hard.

"Yes, yes, and before that Pete caught fish."

"...and before that we passed out of the pleasant esker country."

"Yes," I encouraged, "and before that..."

"...and before that, we had breakfast."

Suddenly, Joe sat bolt upright and stared in horror at my naked body astraddle him.

"George! What are you doing!"

"You are O.K. now, Joe," I said.

"Jesus Christ! George! Get off me!" He pushed me off. His shove was purposeful and with force. Before, when he had been thrashing about, his arms had frequently struck me; but it was as if he was unaware of my presence. He had recognized me at last. I knelt beside him. He looked around the tent, and then at my blanket on top of him, a puzzled expression on his face.

"You're O.K. now," I repeated, fearing that he would retreat into the relative safety of insanity yet again when he realized where he was.

"Where's Art?" he asked.

"Outside," I replied.

"I just had the most terrible dream," he said.

"You're all right now," I said.

He stared at me for a long time, as if he were trying to make sense of things, then he said: "It wasn't a dream, was it?"

"You're O.K. now," I repeated.

"Thanks, George," he finally said, and rolled over on his side. Just before falling into a deep sleep, he mumbled, "You can have all my tobacco, George."

All his tobacco had been lost to the river.

When I came around next [Joe continues], I was surprised to find that I was completely naked and in a tent. I couldn't figure out why this would be. I sat bolt upright. It was dark out. Someone [Peter Franck] thrust a large can under my nose and told me to take five swigs. I did. Then Skip came into the tent, undressed and got into a sleeping bag. After a while, I looked out of the tent. I turned back and casually asked Skip where Art was. He replied that Art was outside. We lay in silence. Finally, I asked what would Art be doing outside. Skip replied, "Art is dead."

From the food supplies which had survived in the red canoe, on the fire he had built out of our emergency sack of driftwood (which we had diligently collected whenever a brook had come down to the river carrying its precious little gifts), Peter had cooked up some corn meal in a tin can and had bent the lid for a spoon. Bruce and I joined Skip and Joe in the tent, and Peter passed the tin can full of hot corn meal to us. We handed the mush first to Joe.

Taking the bent tin lid, Joe made one of his expert scoops and cored a large lump; but instead of gulping it down, he passed it to Bruce on his right. Bruce looked at it, and offered it to Skip. Skip looked at it, and handed it to me.

In the beginning of the trip, I had taken comfort in believing that I would not be the first man to die, because I was in the best physical condition; but now as I stared at the lump of corn meal, I had other desires. I passed the enticing lump back to Joe, who ate it, then Joe passed the whole can of corn meal over to Bruce.

What we had all learned was that there are things more frightening than death. What we passed around that night was more than just a can of lumpy mush. "Take, eat; this is my body which is given for you: do this in remembrance of me."

When the corn meal was gone, Peter passed in a package of Velveeta cheese. I handed it to Skip. He took out Art's hunting knife and sliced the cheese into six equal pieces and then passed them around for us to choose, as was his custom. When the cheese came back to him, he picked up the fifth piece, and we all stared at the sixth remaining piece. Art lay outside. We all wondered if we should bring him into the tent with us and give him his piece of cheese, even though he was now dead.

Finally, Skip divided up the sixth piece: but once again, he divided it into six pieces. Then, at last, he divided up the sixth morsel five ways, and we finished off all the cheese, leaving none for Art.

That night, the five of us huddled into the tiny two-man mountain tent. The shivers and the shakes rolled from one side of the tent to the other as we shared what little warmth remained between us.

In 1913, Norwegian Christian Leden sailed for Hudson Bay (N.W. Territories, Canada) and arranged to live and travel with the Keewatin Eskimos, with the intention of recording the customs and practices of the Eskimos before they were changed by "civilized ways." The following epic, taken from the excellent <u>Across the Keewatin Icefields</u>*, happened during these travels.*

ACROSS THE KEEWATIN ICEFIELDS

by Christian Leden

Excerpts from *Across the Keewatin Icefields* used with Permission of
Watson and Dwyer Publishing Co.

OCTOBER 6

Once more afloat and on our way. A stiff southwest breeze hustles us along. We could not desire a better wind. If it holds we should be able to reach our destination within a week.

At midday the sun peers through the cloud, and I cannot refrain from taking an observation. Before I have sighted it, it vanishes behind the snowy overcast. The medicine man makes a hostile gesture toward the sextant. He seems to mean it.

Towards evening the wind increases and it begins to snow. I call a council of war with Donald and urge him to keep at a greater distance from this dangerous coast lest we run aground again. The medicine man and some others thrust themselves into the debate and object to our steering farther seaward. Donald is plainly unwilling to oppose the wishes of his fellow countrymen and alters the course only very slightly. The Eskimos still feel to their very bones the fright engendered by the last gale from the

October 7

Storm and snow flurries. The sea is once more alarmingly shallow. As a matter of course the Eskimos steered nearer to land during the night, while I was sleeping. These landlubbers! It is devilishly cold to be sailing thus in an open boat. Spray and snow mix to coat the sides of the boat in a thick sheet of ice. Sails and tackle are likewise badly iced. We have all that we can do in beating off the ice as fast as it accumulates lest the boat become heavily encrusted and retard our progress.

A cup of hot coffee or tea would be a blessing, but with the gale blowing hard and the sea running high we cannot heat the water. To grumble is useless. We must be content with cold pemmican, raw meat and ice-cold drinking water. The latter, at least, has not frozen. Our water cask is in the forepart of the boat and the Eskimo women have made a covering of fur for it.

The women are sad today. The mothers of small children have had a desperate time of it. Several are seasick again. During the recent storm they kept remarkably well. Perhaps sheer panic wards off sickness. Wailing children, seasick mothers, ravenous dogs, superstitious sailors, and a medicine man who puts absurd ideas into their heads; all in all a delightful group of travelers. It is the medicine man's certainty that the cause of the gale and snowdrift is my sextant and my sextant alone.

Again the wind has changed, this time to the southeast. In consequence we can sail on for a while with ease, but we are shipping much water and tend steadily towards the land. Are we to repeat our recent adventure? Shall we again somewhere on the coast be tossed about amid shingle, reefs and creaming surf? And a blizzard to add to these? The Eskimos are eager to land again. Old Donald turns his anxious gaze back and forth along the shoreline, seeking any sort of harbor, but with a heavily laden boat it is unthinkable to make one's way to land through shallow water. Our necromancer gives us further counsel: With the exception of food, clothes and weapons we shall heave everything overboard, beginning with my instruments. The outlook for me and my equipment is not rosy. But Donald has the same luck as before; he finds an open navigable channel and steers us in past rocks and pounding surf. The narrow channel conducts us into a small bay. It is a recess surrounded by low heights and hills crowned with boulders. The cove seems perfectly safe, and so we cast anchor.

It is half-tide when we do so. Nonetheless there is a frightful distance between our anchorage and the shore. A few men board a canoe and paddle to land to examine the country. After the lapse of an hour they come back to report that they have found driftwood and a good tenting place.

My double tent remains aboard this time. At sea it was thoroughly drenched with spray and snow and now is frozen stiff as a snowshoe. The skin tents of the Eskimos can put up with more frost before freezing and then they can be made flexible again by beating them. We land with two tents of caribou skin, the required quantity of rations, and cooking and sleeping equipment. Reaching shore is a fresh cause of trouble, for the water is so shallow that the canoes cannot approach the beach. We wade the rest of the way and with long cables moor the canoes to the rocks on shore. Then we wade back to fetch our belongings from the moored canoes. When we are all on dry land we have to drag ourselves 1.5 kilometers back and forth over the shingle to get to the top of a low hill which seemed to promise security even against a high tide.

When we return to fetch the last of our camping equipment we find that the tide has so risen that we have to wade merely to reach the rocks to which our canoes are moored. We haul the canoes close to us, board them to supply the last of our needs and go through the same old ordeal in getting our goods to land. Snow is now falling mixed with rain; we are soon soaked through. I cannot describe what we endured in hauling the articles most essential for camping that same 1.5 kilometers up the beach and in setting up the tents; steeped with salt water inside our clothing and with a snowy pulp clinging to our outer garments, all this done in a cruel wind.

We heap up a mountain of driftwood, melt snow, brew coffee and cook seal meat. By the time the meal is over the tide is already within a few meters of our tents. As the hour of high tide is still some time off we are obliged to look around for a resting place of greater security. By good fortune we find another hill which seems to be a good deal higher than the one we occupy; but we can reach it only by wading knee-deep and by dragging all our baggage through broad encircling waters. The narrow harbour which we fancied that we had entered at ebb tide is changing into a flood rising to form a large bay. Only a few reefs and sandbars separate it from the open sea. All that is left of the land we had seen as we sailed in through the flying snow is a few tiny islets. The mainland is so far off that it cannot be made out through the driving snow. Our present camp is on a tiny island in a broad ocean bay and at flood-tide the water is within five or six meters of our tents.

Darkness is descending by the time the tents are re-pitched; we lie down tired and dripping wet. Okalek takes his turn on watch tonight; the rest of us squeeze, as best we can, into the two tents. My tent-mates are Donald, his wife and a man with a borrowed spouse. During the night the wind snaps a tent pole, and the tent comes down and nearly suffocates us. In the darkness and a raging gale it is impossible to put things right.

The cold is increasing; the storm is driving fine snow into our shelter. As I lie in the half-open tent and try desperately to dry my clothes with the warmth of my body I think of the two surveyors, lying at this moment, warm and dry, in the Churchill police barracks. The words of the older one come back to me: "I don't envy the young Norwegian." No, indeed!

OCTOBER 8

At the glimpse of dawn we rise, shake the snow from our sleeping gear and wriggle from under the collapsed tent. Donald borrows my axe, trims the broken end of the tent pole and binds the break with sealskin thong. Then we set up the tent again. Illatnak fetches some driftwood, kindles a fire at the tent door and puts on my coffee kettle. Soon the tent is so full of smoke that my eyes are running and I am gasping for air. I can no longer endure it inside. With a bold leap I vault over the kettle and fire and out into the fresh air. But it is bitter cold out there, especially in my damp clothing. I cannot tell how many degrees of frost it is, for my meteorological instruments are lying safely packed on the boat. Had I brought them along the rough usage they would have undergone in yesterday's landing would have destroyed them.

I call at the other tent: There children, wives and grandmothers are crawling out of bed. Only Laughing Boy and the medicine man are on their feet. They are gathering driftwood and making the same preparations for cooking as Donald and Illatnak are just opposite. And so I am homeless. How can these Eskimos endure such smoke? Their eyes are always more or less inflamed from the habit of cooking in the tent over driftwood, willow and moss.

I wish that these landlubbers were under sail again instead of loafing in this miserable spot. The wind has veered around to the northwest and this is usually a sign that it will soon fall calm. But the Eskimos have no thought of setting out today. Since our adventure, when the boat was almost swamped, they have grown very nervous. Donald predicts the approach of another gale from the northeast. The stretch of coast just ahead of us is particularly dangerous.

In the course of the day the wind sweeps vast quantities of snow onto the little fragment of our island which remains dry at high tide. I am at a loss to know where all the snow drift comes from—so far from the mainland. Laughing Boy boards a canoe and paddles off to hunt. He soon comes back with a seal, and now for a real feast. From morning till evening my good Eskimos do nothing but cook and eat and are in vastly better humour. As long as they have a roof over their heads and something in the pot that they can digest, they are content and take no thought for the morrow.

October 9

Today at last I succeed in goading the Eskimos to moving on. The boat is so ice-encrusted that we spend much time in making it seaworthy. The tackle is frozen so stiff that a man climbs up the mast to loosen it and make it workable. The sails too are stiff; much time is lost in hoisting them.

The sky is clear with a fine breeze from the west. It is much easier to get out of this harbour than it was, the day before yesterday, to find our way in. The west wind reduces the swell caused by the recent storm. It is soon calm enough to permit us to light a fire in the cooking stove. Later the wind grows stronger; we sail rapidly with the sea foaming at the bow.

We are cheered by the bright sunshine. Perhaps we may yet reach Chesterfield Inlet before the sea freezes. I must take advantage of a clear sky to take a sun shot and determine exactly where we are. Furtively I grope in my instrument case in the hope of fishing out my sextant at a moment when no one is looking. But the master magician is eyeing me sideways following every movement I make. Scarcely have I opened the case and laid my hand on the sextant when he murmurs an incantation and makes so hideous a face that all men look at me as though I were Satan, here to cannibalize their children. Even Donald, who normally seems less superstitious than the rest, appears grave and worried. So I slam the chest shut and try to give the impression that I had been merely checking my instruments to make sure that they had not suffered damage in the recent foul weather.

About one o'clock we are sitting down to drink coffee when the sun is hidden by dark, threatening clouds. Until that moment we had not observed a single cloud and were reckoning on sunlight until evening. At the same time the wind dies away and the sails dangle slackly from the yards. We look at one another surprised and uneasy; the medicine man makes a few expressive gestures and cries: "Tornrak!" (The evil spirit). He is delirious and deadly pale. In a moment the wind springs up again, fills the sails with resounding smacks and whistles through the rigging as if all the devils from Hell were holding a concert aloft. Donald throws his cup away and, jumping up, roars a few sharp orders. In an instant the men are hauling on the mainsail. It is no easy matter to lower it when it is all stiff with frost. One or two violent gusts strike in an interval of a few seconds before the dance really begins. "Take in all sail," shouts Donald. A mere rag, the smallest sail on the boat, remains hoisted. The rest of the sails and everything else that is not riveted or nailed down is covered right across with a weight of tarpaulins and lashed fast, for now we are in real trouble. No one had noticed from what quarter the first squall came; it seemed to blow from all directions.

Presently, both mast and hull are cracking. The compass dances around the dial in sympathy with the storm. For a while it blows from the southeast and then wheels to the northeast. The wind hollows out troughs in the sea and rolls up waves mountains high. Donald snatches the tiller away from Okalek. We all peer anxiously towards the land though well aware that no port is to be found here. We are in genuine distress; the boat is beginning to take in water. The Eskimos are speechless. Their only hope is in Donald, and the goddess of the sea. Donald is shivering with cold and fright. The storm has over-taken us in a most difficult channel.

As long as it is in any way possible I keep on writing in my diary in the hope of keeping myself calm and setting others an example of composure. Only two men at a time can work the pump and Donald, our best seaman, will trust no one else with the tiller. The others can only sit until their turn at the pump comes round again. The sky grows darker. Snow comes thicker and thicker; soon we can barely see two boat lengths ahead. The roar of wind and sea is deafening. Near us yawns an abyss; at the same moment a great wave breaks on board, bowls myself and others over on top of the freight; one or two are all but washed overboard. We clutch at the lashings of the tarpaulin covering the cargo, and hang on for dear life. Another wave strikes; the boat is heaved up and thrown over on its side—and by a miracle the greater part of the water shipped is spilled over-board again. It all happens in a matter of seconds. Drenched with brine without and wet to the bone, we take turns at the pump and toil with an energy which only those who are fighting for their lives can sustain.

The sea boils and foams; in the raging storm it raises a mist of spray. Another great wave comes thundering over us. Aground on a shoal! This is the end. A shriek from the women pierces one to the marrow. The waves smash against the boat and shake it like raging demons. It is lifted up and shot forward as if by an explosion of dynamite. We are back in deep water, and working the pump as if possessed. The boat is still afloat—but for how long?

SHIPWRECK
OCTOBER 11

In sodden fur garments we fight the strength of despair. In bliz-zard and darkness, and burdened with chests and furs, we painfully seek a way over rock-strewn shallows through surf and spray from the wreck to a bleak and forbidding shore. Side by side, fight a life-and-death battle against the merciless forces of Nature.

The surf roars and the gale pitilessly lashes our tortured eyes with driving snow pellets. We toil under our burdens, through the unceasing pounding of the waves over smooth and slippery rock; bruised and bloody from stumbling, we always recover and labour ever forwards.

The grey dawn glimmers and puts an end to that night of horror; the throng, hungry and almost dead from exhaustion, clench their teeth and renew the fight—eight hours long and without intermission.

Most of the provisions have been lost overboard. Much of the equipment was ruined even before the little boat, after a long and bitter struggle, was lifted up by a colossal wave and tossed into her last anchorage.

The scanty remains of food and equipment are treated with as much reverential piety as if they were the Communion Cup and the Host. When the last pieces have been brought to land and stacked in a dismal heap, sails and tarpaulins are drawn over them and carefully weighted down with stones.

With superhuman exertions we try to haul the wreck out of the surf and onto the beach. Only one anchor remains and it is the smaller one. The larger anchor with its stout cable lies far out on the sea bottom in the lee of an islet—a silent witness to the irresistible force of wind and waves.

The numerous holes in the boat's bottom and on one side are proof that she struck several times until she was hurled with a mighty crash onto the mainland.

With thongs of walrus hide made fast to a rock we tow the wreck to land. Foaming like the devil's slavering tongue, the surf sweeps high up the beach as if it would devour the last remnant of the pitiful wreck. It is finished at last, and all that remains of boat and lading has been rescued. Hungry and mortally tired, the men drag themselves into the skin tents.

Inside lie a few primitive weapons and the wretched remains of household furnishings. Skins and caribou-skin blankets, all frozen stiff and full of snow, must serve as bedding. Speechless forms sit in a circle and beat frozen caribou hides with pieces of driftwood and bones. The shattered ice crusts rise in little clouds of frosty dust; the skins become pliable and are spread out to be used a blankets. Men and women, young and old, creep under the covers, snuggled together for mutual warmth. At one end of the plank floor which serves as the community sleeping area a few children and old women are lying. They have slept already for some hours as they could render no help at the wreck outside in the battle with the roaring surf.

Soon all consciousness of sorrow and pain pass away in long, deep slumber; my brain alone is yet wide awake, and working feverishly, despite the weariness of my limbs. Is this really the end? Cast away on a barren shore, uninhabited, thousands of miles from the civilized world. Provisions saved, enough for a week or two; a few firearms and instruments.

Everything else that I called my own sunk in the depths of the sea. This is the fruit of all my toils and struggles, the reward for a thousand anxieties and deprivations!

Hopeless and helpless. Only fools revolt against the decrees of fate. Why live and suffer torment? What for? Why fight so stubbornly for life? Why do you struggle so stubbornly when the waves, like ravening lions, would overwhelm you? Why do you not fling yourself into the arms of the hungry sea? Instead with roving eye and almost in despair you try to spy out a harbor while the mighty hurricane roars around you and the end may come any moment. Death at your side beckons and promises relief from your sorrows; you sweat away at the pump to keep the boat afloat. Why? Because you yearn to live—and with reason; so many hopes remain that would bring you to fulfillment. But now, after an almost miraculous escape from death, life seems without purpose. How will you accomplish the purpose which has brought you to this extremity? Your equipment lies at the bottom of the sea, and what little remains is battered and little better than junk! The game is lost and over!

The evil One lurks in the gloom with savage grin.

O Great Almighty Power deliver me from this sorrow.

At last sleep comes like a pitying angel, and so to the fevered mind a face, divinely comforting, appears again and blesses the poor dreamer with a smile of indescribable sweetness.

SHELTERLESS
OCTOBER 9

Last night about eleven o'clock the screams of women and the howling of dogs plucked me suddenly from the sweetest of dreams and awoke me to bitter reality. Donald's tent had been leveled by the fury of the gale and lay crumpled over our heads. Several times in the course of the night we tried in vain to set it up again. The blizzard still rages with undiminished force. Phew! That's a dog's life! The snow lies in the tent half a meter deep. Time and again through the night I had to get up and shake off the snow lest I be buried alive.

　　Soon the storm will have been raging for three days, and as
yet there is no sign of its abating. We are all as hungry as
wolves, and half of us are roofless owing to the accident of
Donald's tent. In addition, in the turmoil of the night I lost my
mitts. They lie somewhere buried under the snow and are no
more to be seen. Going to bed last night I laid them beside my
sleeping bag; but they were so wet that they soon froze as hard
as a stone. When I got up in the night to shake off the snow they
were pushed aside and, no doubt, trampled into the snow. We
burrowed around in it, and dug up every hard object but found
nothing except stones. In such wind and cold it is torture to be
moving about without mitts. My Eskimo dress has not a single
pocket in which to bury my hands. In any case, since the wreck I
have certainly other things to do than to move about with my
hands in my pockets. Donald's wife will make me a new pair if I
supply the proper materials. Caribou hide it must be, she says;
other skins, especially that of seal, are not warm enough for the
winter. I have nothing in the way of hide except my dog skin
sleeping bag and my old sealskin dress. But they are of no help
to me. Unlike caribou hide, frozen sealskin cannot be made flexible by beating it; it freezes bone-hard. Donald's wife is perfectly right; I know from my own experience what it is like to travel
abroad in sealskin that is frozen stiff. If I get into my sleeping
bag, my sealskin garments thaw and I am soaked with moisture
all night; scarcely have I crawled out of my bag, and my clothing begins to grow as stiff as a board. But I cannot go to bed
without my skin clothing, for it then freezes so hard overnight
that in the morning I cannot put it on. In this cold weather I will
not venture to move about in Adam's dress, and so have no
choice but to wear my sealskin clothes day and night until I can
get proper winter clothing of caribou hide.
　　At noon Donald comes back tired and exhausted. In spite of
the frightful weather he has gone some distance along the beach
to look for driftwood — but without success. Yet he has fetched
some old putrid seal meat from our caches by the wreck. It had
been classed as dog food. But, hungry and faint as we are, we
eat it ourselves, rotten, raw and hard-frozen. When in want the

Devil eats flies! When Donald learns that the mitts I have lost in the snow are still not recovered, and that I have no material for a new pair, he says, "Poalukrangitok okkiomi, Pitauangitok, illa," (To be without mitts in winter is utter misery.) With these words the good old man tears a piece of caribou hide out of his undergarment and begs his wife to make me mitts with it.

By now the winter has begun in earnest. In any case we would have been stranded somewhere along this coast even if we had not suffered the shipwreck. The Eskimos say that as soon as the wind goes down the seashore will be lined with ice.

From now until July of next year we have only one means of transportation—the komatik. A piece of luck that dogs and komatiks have been saved. However, for the present, we just stay where we are, until the larger rivers are frozen over, and the snow cover is at least deep enough to smooth over the gravel ridges. We must make the best of it in our camp here and count ourselves lucky that at least the shipwreck has not cost any lives.

The worst of it is that we have lost all our clothes and winter equipment—except for what we had on at the moment of the shipwreck. For my part, I was wearing my summer clothing of netserk (spotted sealskin), which is utterly useless for winter wear. The Eskimos are not much better off. When the frightful storm took us by surprise they too were in summer wear, that is, old clothes stored up from the previous winter. The spoils of the summer hunt, caribou skins, out of which winter clothing would be made, are, for the most part lost.

My double tent and the other pitiful relics of my equipment are lying frozen hard under tarpaulin and stones near the wreck. I am without shelter and have nothing to eat. To begin with, Donald's tent cannot be set upright, for some of the tent poles are broken. To be sure, the Eskimos have set up other tents, but they are even smaller than Donald's. In consequence both tents are fearfully crowded.

Now that Donald's wife has sewn me a pair of mitts, my next care is to fetch up tent, provisions and ammunition from the beach. This is hateful work in such a fearful blizzard. The way from our camping place to the wreck and the heap of salvaged belongings is a long one.

None of the Eskimos shows the least inclination to accompany me in this foul weather and help to bring up my tent. Without aid I cannot tear open the frost-hardened tarpaulin and roll away the heavy stones with which my tent and the rest of our goods are covered. Without help I can do nothing and I exert all my powers of persuasion to arouse someone for the task. At last Illatnak declares himself willing to come and help in exchange for a pound of sugar. Perhaps he hopes that his borrowed wife will be doubly amiable and obliging if sweetened with sugar.

The torments that we endured in making our way through the whirling blizzard to my belongings beside the wreck and in loosening the frozen stones and tarpaulin are beyond description. And yet they were nothing compared to the agony of the journey back to camp. Then gale and snowdrift drive into our faces taking our breath away. Laden with the tent we drag ourselves, step by step, forward over the ice-covered shingle. Every few moments we have to drop the tent and turn our back to the gale, in order again to draw breath. Time and again the blast lays us flat on the smooth stones and more than once we almost break neck and legs or crush our ribs. Our eyes smart unbearably from the driving snow with which the raging hurricane lashes our faces. We can see a few paces ahead; we have to stumble over the shingly beach to find the camp. The surf has so churned up the beach that I fancy myself on a battlefield furrowed with trenches. It is over ground like that that we haul the tent in the teeth of the gale.

Hours pass and we are still far from our objective. The tide is rising and spewing its foam over the beach. We must end our course inland and try to steer by the direction of the wind. But it now appears that deprived of water and beach as plumb-line we are going astray. So, back to the shingle on the shore!

Illatnak chooses this moment to pretend we are lost, and drops the tent. He asserts that it is impossible to reach the camp before nightfall if we continue to drag the frozen tent. I refuse to listen. If he is not man enough to stay with me and bring in the tent, then I am resolved to do it alone. My scorn makes not the least impression on him. Besides I can hardly make good my boast. I am simply incapable of hauling it over the bumpy shingle and then dragging it further towards lands. Illatnak comes back and vows that the tent must be left to lie where it is, for we must make all haste to get to camp lest darkness overtake us on the way. I bid him "go." I remain with the tent. I have a feeling that I will never see the tent again, if I leave it here to the mercy of the blizzard. In that case I am shelterless for good and all and quite at the mercy of the Eskimos. "Kappearnnnnakonni" (You need not worry), says Illatnak; and tries to persuade me that to remain alone in the storm is certain death. "Kaovimangitoalni" (You will not listen to me), he adds in a threatening tone. I tug away at the tent until almost dead with exhaustion. In spite of wind and frost, sweat is trickling down under my clothes and the frozen sealskin dress takes on another crust of ice. I can scarcely hold myself upright under my burden.

At last Illatnak seems to relent—perhaps my perseverance has won his respect. Seeing no hope of coaxing me away from my tent, he too lays hold of it once more.

Again we toil ahead together, as best we can. Darkness comes down on us; we shout at the top of our voices hoping that an answering hail from the camp will give us direction. No. No reply. Only louder roaring of the wind. We stagger forward, and again shout—now we bellow loud enough to burst an artery. At last an answering shout from the Eskimo camp. After a short interval Okalek comes to our aid and together we bring the tent over the short remaining space to the camp.

Four of us toil in storm and darkness to set up my tent, and I actually am in possession of a home of my own. I fetch sleeping bag, firearms and camera from Donald's tumbled tent. I am to have the pleasure of enjoying an evening by myself in rest and quiet. But destiny rules otherwise; it very soon appears that the tent is uninhabitable. The gale drives in the snow freely as if the tent door were mosquito netting. I can find no remedy; the snow drives in heaps. It comes in as fast as I can sweep it out. All my effort wasted. I am in the same plight as at Churchill when I was trying to drain off the water.

The outer tent is missing. We must have left it lying under the tarpaulin by the wreck. The smaller inner tent by itself was too heavy for us. It is quite out of the question to live in my tent without its outer covering. A skin tent is to be preferred to the ordinary canvas tent.

So I must again seek shelter with the Eskimos. In the morning I shall find a helper and bring up the outer tent, and again have privacy and comfort. The Eskimo tent is occupied in every corner; but in Laughing Boy's skin tent I find a little recess between fat woman and the sorcerer. The latter appears to be uneasy and snuggles up to the mother-in-law.

Some hours before dawn Laughing Boy gets up to start a fire and cook tainted seal meat. Yesterday was kind to him; despite the snowy tempest, he found a quantity of driftwood. In a moment the tent is so full of smoke that I am almost choked. Because of the blizzard the tent is so tightly sealed that the smoke finds no outlet; unlike the Indian teepee the Eskimo tent has no outlet in the roof. The smoke fills the whole space and must find its own way out — if it can. When cooking is going on one has to choose between choking inside or freezing in the open air. He who has not experienced it cannot conceive what a hell smoke can make of a Padliermiut tent. Smarting eyes and impaired respiration are the most frightful torment.

I leap up as if bitten by a scorpion and dash out of the tent, with Laughing Boy's guffaw resounding behind me. Better to freeze outside in the gale. But the change is too abrupt; to creep out moist and steaming from a sleeping bag, and dash out headlong into driving snow. My sealskin dress, thawed out overnight and damp, stiffens at once into ice. But I soon find work which sets my blood circulating.

I borrow from Donald a primitive snow shovel made of driftwood, and go over to shovel out my tent. Having been unoccupied all night it is almost full of snow. I work for hours without pause. By daybreak I have done the job in rough. In the meantime the wind has veered to the northwest and is diminishing slightly. So now not much fresh snow will drift in.

I am just finished with my task when Laughing Boy calls me to breakfast, which is tainted, half-cooked seal meat. In spite of my hunger, I have no relish for it. If I have to gulp down bad meat, I greatly prefer it to be raw and frozen. The smell is less offensive and it seems less repulsive than when thawed and half-cooked. I shall never learn to like such delicacies from an Eskimo kitchen. My appetite is quickly satisfied by the smell alone.

After this so-called breakfast we go down with the children and other stray persons to our belongings stacked by the wreck. In the camp we have nothing to eat except rotten seal meat.

The gale, after blowing for four days, is now, in the opinion of the Eskimos, drawing to an end. So we must make the most of today in carrying the needed food and other baggage to the camp before another storm comes up. Digging out our property is naturally a most troublesome task. Half of it is buried meters deep under a drift. The large stones which are lying on the pile are frozen down and refuse to be dislodged. In that night of horror we had rolled the stones onto the pile that the storm might not blow the tarpaulin off and, not improbably, whirl away our possessions with it. The outer tent lies close to the top under its own tarpaulin, which also covers my instruments. Only a few meteorological instruments have suffered damage. Groping beside it, I dig out an ammunition chest — in the best of condition, thanks to the airtight and watertight container. Other items come to light; a chest of matches labeled 'stinker' now becomes of immense value; some 23-liter canisters of petroleum; one of my Swedish primus stoves; a lamp; the tool box. The moving picture camera is saved but has taken a hard knock and its tripod is lost. The phonograph is there, but it does not seem ready for immediate use. Only a few boxes of blank records turn up, and of film tape a little more than 600 meters remain. The chest of chemicals for developing film is undamaged, for, like the ammunition chest, it is airtight and watertight. Only a few pairs of skis remain. I had previously saved two pairs and carefully guarded them, but one of them along with other items has disappeared without a trace in the most miraculous manner. Some sugar and sweet chocolate are still edible, thanks to the packing and the same is true of the chest of pemmican and half a chest of edibles from the Army & Navy, London. We had eaten the other half on the voyage.

The rest of the magnificent provisions supplied by the Army & Navy is lost — apart from the boxes which, owing to the lack of space in the boat, I had been compelled to leave behind at Churchill in the care of the fur trader. My pipes, a carton of Craven tobacco mixture and another of Capstan's Navy Cut will be a great comfort to me in the wilderness.

Some sugar and other such wares, which the trader had given us, are also saved. But, as they were not well enough packed for so hazardous a voyage, they are almost all spoilt. My own sugar, in airtight and watertight metal containers with double tops and bottoms, and packed in stout wooden boxes, has escaped without damage. The trader's sugar was packed in light boxes lined with paper.

The Eskimos take possession of the half-ruined foodstuffs furnished by the trader. Laughing Boy excels in long and supple fingers. I have no desire to 'sweeten' my tea with sugar that has been steeped in ocean brine, but the Eskimos seem to enjoy salted sugar. Could our fur trader have foreseen what happened to us, he would probably have given freely to the Eskimos spoiled goods and repaid himself with arctic foxes and other tobacco products.

I take as much of my own goods as it is possible to haul. We carefully spread tarpaulins over the rest and weight them down with stones. We have to drag our loads a terrible distance. Later, when more snow has fallen and the rough shingle is well covered, we shall shift our camp this way and build snow houses. Now I am glad to have brought up the inner tent yesterday, for without that we have more than enough to carry on our backs.

Now for the first time we perceive the frightful chaos caused by the storm. Deep trenches have been gouged out along the beach and between them are tangled masses of seaweed and sea-grass which the sea has vomited up along the tide-line and a good way up the shore.

On our way back the Eskimos discover footprints — fresh, but half drifted in — near the place where we had stowed our goods. The sorcerer assures us that these tracks are nothing but the footprints of Tornrak the Devil; we are unconvinced. I think it is possible that there may be other people nearby — the wild inland Eskimos, for instance. But the medicine man shakes his head and declares that at this time of year people never come down to the coast and that the tracks can only be those of the Devil or some other spirit.

The wind dies away in the late afternoon. Clear sky appears. I make haste to set up my outer tent to be prepared for the next blizzard which may come at any time. Then I put a pipe in my mouth, start the primus stove and prepare a feast of joy and thanksgiving because I once more have my own roof overhead. I am grateful to Fate for leaving me at least something. With a little economy I can make my half-chest of Army & Navy Stores last four weeks instead of fourteen days. In addition I have my Krag carbine and some ammunition. The last jar of dried fruit — apricot, currant — I break up and cook into sauce. There is also an English plum pudding with brandy sauce, but this must be put by for some other time. My prize possession is Thornes pemmican.

As I am rising from my first good meal to fill my pipe, I have the greatest surprise of my life. I pluck at my beard to assure myself that I am awake and in my right mind. Is it a ghost? Or has the first good meal after several days of hunger and stress gone to my head? 'Tom Thumb' is standing dimly lighted at the tent door and grinning at me. I lay hold of a boot and pull it out to throw at the ghost. The figure at the door jumps to one side and cries, 'Kappearna!' (Distress).

He is flesh and blood, he is Kubluk, Tom Thumb himself and not a ghost at all. The little fellow is a Netschillingmiut Eskimo with whom I had formed a casual friendship. Three weeks prior to my departure he had left Churchill with a number of inland Eskimos and a mixed-blood in the employ of the Hudson's Bay Company. He was to carry word to the Company trader at the northern post that the expected schooner would not arrive and to bring him some provisions and trade goods for the winter. Tom Thumb by rights should have been a least 250 kilometers north of here. What can his appearance mean here?

He seems very dejected, hungry and frost-bitten. He is wearing a tourist's summer cap, the gift sometime ago of a whaler; otherwise he is clothed in ragged caribou skin; a pair of canvas trousers, obtained from the trader at Churchill; stockings and Indian moccasins apparently once belonging to a mixed-blood, and a worn-out policeman's tunic which presumably he had picked up at Churchill. He carries also a rusty old Winchester rifle, a dozen cartridges and a large pannah, the kind of knife used in building stone houses. Where does he come from and where is he going?

I serve him coffee and pemmican of which he devoured three times a normal portion. When at last he is finished eating he produces a little leather pouch which he carries between his shirt and jacket, hung from his neck with a light thong. From this he takes out a dirty piece of paper bearing a penciled scrawl which he begs me to read.

'STORM AND FOUL WEATHER. SHIPWRECK. BOAT TOTALLY WRECKED. CARGO LOST. HELP AT ONCE OR SOON DEAD OF HUNGER AND COLD.'

The note had been written by the mixed-blood and was addressed to the Churchill trader. The boat that left Churchill three weeks in advance of mine had been driven ashore on the very same night as ourselves. I held in my hand the despairing cry of the Company's mixed-blood servant. He has ordered the little chap to travel the long road to Churchill on shank's mare. Truly a naive idea; but what will not a desperate man try when death is clutching at him? Even if Tom Thumb could have actually reached Churchill (but that was impossible, for he could not swim across the numerous rivers between here and his destination) the fur trader could send no help until the rivers were frozen and passable by dogsled. The mixed-blood would have died of hunger long before that.

In answer to my question, 'How could he hope to cross the rivers?' Tom replies: 'Ammiasuk,' (I don't know). He tells me that the mixed-blood had so constantly badgered and scolded him to fetch help from Churchill that he wearied of his everlasting nagging, shouldered his gun and set out hoping that the rivers would soon freeze and the snow be firm enough for the building of houses, and that he perhaps might reach Churchill, if he found enough wildlife on the way, and could support himself by hunting. The two inland Eskimos, he adds, were no longer with the mixed-blood. Soon after the shipwreck they had packed up their belongings and gone their own way.

The mixed-blood is sitting alone with his Indian wife, expecting help from Churchill. Poor Devil! If he looks for help from the quarter, he will wait a long time. It was a piece of luck that my Eskimos and I came to grief when we did. Perhaps we might yet rescue him and his wife. It is lucky for him that Kubluk did not pass here before the storm ended. In that case he would not have seen our tents nor have suspected that he was passing a camp. Had he begun his journey earlier, according to the mixed-blood's wish, it is a hundred to one that he would never have seen us. The mixed-blood is waiting, Tom says, only half day's journey — 14-17 kilometers away from us. He has food for four days, sigalah (biscuits), and tukto-nerki (caribou meat). A few days before the shipwreck the inland Eskimos went ashore and killed a caribou.

I beg Tom to go back as fast as he could bearing victuals and a letter from me inviting the mixed-blood to join our camp. I promise to share my supplies with him, and to see to it that he should go to Churchill by dogsled as soon as the rivers freeze and the snow is firm enough for the construction of snowhouses.

The ensuing days were a severe test. More blizzards blew up, lasting for entire days, with short intermittent breathing spaces between them. It was difficult in the short period between storms to travel the long route from camp to the cache by the wreck and replenish our stores in the camp.

The dogs were no help to us for the snow cover was too thin to afford a passage for komatiks over the rock-strewn terrain. A blizzard normally lasted three days without a break. On the second day it generally blew from the northwest or north. It was then at its worst, and it was impossible to remain in open air for more than a few seconds. On the third day it veered to the northwest and slackened a little. If necessary, we could then venture outside the tent and do odd jobs — provided that we wore full winter dress. But in our insufficient clothing we suffered frightfully in the bitter cold, when necessity forced us to leave the shelter of the tent on a stormy day. The Eskimos and, above all, the dogs, were often hungry. My daily journal might perhaps furnish some idea of the sort of life we led and the hard times we endured the first weeks after the shipwreck.

OCTOBER 14

Another blizzard; it woke me up at five in the morning by shaking the tent in an alarming manner. Steaming with warmth and perspiration I rise from my sleeping bag to save my roof while there is yet time. With moist body and garments frozen stiff I struggle for three hours and finally make the tent secure. That makes me hungry. After breakfast we take our rifles and, despite the weather, go on a caribou hunt.

A short distance inland we separate and spread out in different directions. The luck of one Eskimo is good; he brings in a young caribou as a trophy. Fresh meat is a great luxury after such a period of hunger. But a small caribou does not go far with so many mouths; twenty half-starved people devour the carcass in a single meal.

For our poor famished dogs little or nothing remains.

OCTOBER 15

The snowstorm has become a blizzard and rages more violently
than ever. Living in tents at this time of year daily becomes
more unbearable. But for the building of snowhouses we must
have more firmer snow.

The blizzard brings us no fresh snow. On the contrary it drives the old snow out to sea in devouring ravenous fury. The
roaring sea thunders on the shore threatening to churn it into a
mash. While this lasts there is no hope of the sea freezing. While
I sit in my tent and write these words the frost is biting my fin-
gertips but I must be sparing with my petroleum; I use the
primus stove for no other purpose than to melt snow and prepare
meals. The dogs are howling from hunger and cold; it is a heart-
rending sound, like a human cry of pain. They try to break into
our tents and fall upon our own scant supply of food. Would that
the weather were such that we could go caribou hunting! We are
in urgent need of fresh meat and fat — for both ourselves and
the dogs.

OCTOBER 16

Now the storm has abated a little. We go hunting. This time it is
Illatanak whom luck favors, and he brings home a caribou. The
men do not seem to value much the skins of the recently killed
caribou; I beg them for my own use to make myself a pair of
trousers. I cannot endure to go abroad in bitter weather in my
old outworn summer trousers. The Eskimos eye me and seem to
ask, 'Is the white man out of his mind?'

I bundle up my skins, go to Donald and beg his wife to sew
me a pair of winter trousers. She shakes her head and makes no
end of excuses. After a long debate Donald informs me that no
Eskimo would cut the skins or sew them; for in their religion it
is a grievous sin to make anything out of the winter coat of a
caribou. Despite this rebuff I go around the camp and try to cor-
rupt the Eskimo women, one after another, to sin against their

religion. Winter clothing of caribou skin, I really must have —
regardless of sin, religion and the sorcerer. But the Eskimos
remain obdurate. They themselves would rather die of cold than
disobey their ancient religion law.

What resources are left to me? Quite unskilled in tailoring I
must set myself to the task. But it is almost impossible to force
the needle through the hide; it is too thick, and the matted hair
makes the work doubly difficult. The Eskimos are watching me.
Before long one of them approaches me with friendly advice not
to waste any more time on my foolish endeavor. Supposing I did
manage to make a pair of trousers I would get no joy out of
them. With a garment made from the long-haired, heavy winter
hide one could not exert himself, even in the bitterest cold, without sweating. That explains it all; in this religion of frost one
must be protected from perspiring. But my well-meaning coun-
selor had an even weightier argument; by continuing my work I
would incur enmity, not only that of the sorcerer, but I would
also grievously offend everyone. For what I am doing is a
twofold sin. Not only is cutting and working of winter hide of
the caribou forbidden by the native religion, but also it is sacri-
lege to sew new clothes of caribou skin in a tent. All that is permitted inside a tent is to make clothes of sealskin and to repair
old garments of caribou hide. In case of necessity it might be
permitted to work on the stuff of an old garment into another
form. For instance, Donald's wife had made me mitts from her
husband's underclothing — that was no sin. But to make new
garments out of caribou hide one must be sitting in a snowhouse
built on the ice of salt water. Always something new to learn! In
any case I must, for the present, give up hope of new winter
clothing of caribou skin. There is no help for it; I must go on
freezing in my sealskin trousers.

OCTOBER 17

At last a fine day — and fine for all of the day! As the wind dies
down Hudson Bay begins to freeze along the shoreline. In late
afternoon the ice already stretches seawards two or three kilo-

meters. I take advantage of the fine weather to fetch from the cache on the beach up to the camp everything I need — pemmican, petroleum, biscuits and a few instruments.

In the afternoon the Eskimo called Beik, whose tent we had observed on the shore during our voyage, joined us. He came with five dogs harnessed to his komatik and will continue north to hunt caribou. His entire baggage amounts to a sleeping bag and a little skin tent. He cannot carry anything more along with the game he kills; the snow is not yet deep enough for a fully loaded komatik. Beik had found a few caribou farther south. But when he learns of our luck hunting to the north of here he resolves to make camp hereabouts with his brother's family, as soon as sledging conditions permit it, and the small river which lies between his camping place and ours is sufficiently frozen to be crossed with a heavy load on his sledge.

Beik is active and alert. On his way to our camp he found the body of a whale swept up onto the land. Presumably it was tossed on shore by the furious waves during the storm which wrecked our boat, for it lay well above the tidemark. Foxes were swarming about the carcass; the place was a sumptuous feast for the predators. Beik stayed there a few days and set up four traps. In a couple of days he caught about thirty foxes, a catch worth a good $1,800; so Beik, his wife and daughters can buy handkerchiefs and resplendent beads, as soon as the snow is deep enough for them to sledge southwards to the fur trader. Later Beik intends to catch more terriganiak (foxes), feasting on the whale carcass. But first he must travel to the north and kill some caribou..

OCTOBER 18

Seven days have passed since the shipwreck. When I recall all that I have suffered in a single week, it seems to me that I have been here a year and a day. I breathe out steam which coats the tent walls so thick with hoarfrost that it resembles the fleece of a sheep.

OCTOBER 19

Again a blizzard, the worst yet; it is drifting through the tent wall and the space between outer and inner tent is packed full of snow. The double tent is a wonderful invention! The fury of the storm exhausts itself on the outer wall; no snow has yet sifted into the inner tent. So in a raging gale and driving snow my living room and sleeping bag remain dry. But for the outer tent it would be unendurable.

Until the storm blows itself out to some degree I am a prisoner within four walls. This time I have at least, all the petroleum and pemmican I need, and can cook and eat as much as I wish. So I am teaching myself to cook; at one time I regretted not having brought with me a cook or kitchen helper. Now I am thankful for having something to do which employs my thoughts. Cooking is the finest diversion that can be imagined when the blizzard imprisons one in a tent. The man who is his own cook and butler has little time for brooding on the miseries of life.

OCTOBER 20

Today, on the third day, the storm as usual moderates a little, and I can again work outside. In the fine weather a few days back I had been able to fetch up some instruments, including two thermometers which had survived the shipwreck. One of them is unusable; the other I dug out of a drift several meters deep, and now put it in the open air. It registers -19 degrees Celsius. That is quite a comfortable temperature in this region; with clothing adapted to the climate and a little artificial heat at mealtimes and the hours of sleep, one can put up with it quite pleasantly. But to one like myself; in old summer clothing, half-damp and half-frozen, made of sealskin, who lacks the means of heating the tent, it can be very uncomfortable at -19 degrees Celsius of frost. Especially when I am sitting still and writing up the journal.

The primus cooker does not suffice as a stove in this wind and cold. Besides I have not enough petroleum to use it for heating purposes. In late afternoon it grows calm. While I am taking my evening meal Tom Thumb reappears. The shipwrecked mixed-blood sends me a letter by him, begging me to send him some provisions, 'the best, not spoiled' from the fur trader's provisions. I give him some of my provisions and bid him tell the mixed-blood to come to our camp immediately.

OCTOBER 21

Very mild weather; only -12 degrees Celsius; quite calm too. The finest weather we have had since our journey began.

Today at last the mixed-blood came. He could not have hoped for better weather at this time of year. He tells us that he has seen a herd of caribou 10 or 11 kilometers north from here, indeed he insists that he met fifteen hundred head. They have begun their southwest trek. That means that winter is upon us in grim earnest. Woe to him who is not clothed warmly enough!

OCTOBER 22

Calm again today. Two consecutive days of fine weather are a real event. The temperature varied a very little today, about -20 degrees Celsius. In the night there was a moderately heavy snowfall, and it seems as if there might soon be more. All to the good — for we shall have good snow for komatik travel. We hope to be building snowhouses fairly soon. Living in tents is no longer endurable.

I suggest that we men all go north to hunt caribou today; but the caribou herd seen yesterday by the mixed-blood tempts my Eskimos not at all. It is not worth the trouble, they say, to go north and haul the kill a long way back. The caribou will come south within range of our rifles. 'Wait a few days, and the caribou will come to us.' That reminds me of an East Greenland Eskimo who tracked a polar bear over the frozen sea, but would not kill him a long way from the settlement. He saved himself the trouble hauling his kill in the simplest manner in the world; he drove the bear before him to the camping ground. When Bruin grew tired of this and turned to his pursUer, he threw his spear at the animal and drove him again. He gradually carried his prey to camp on the prey's own legs and killed him, so to say, on the threshold of his own snowhoUse.

In the heat of the chase the European would naturally have killed him as soon as he had him at gun's point and would have only taken thought of the labor of carrying his 'bag' home after the event. But the Eskimos are a practical people, and avoid hazards and unnecessary exertion.

Besides Tom Thumb and the mixed-blood, the two inland Eskimos who were in the mixed-blood's company have now joined us. The mysterious footprints near the cache on the beach which my comrades supposed to be those of Tornrak, doubtless were those of inland Eskimos. One of these men seems scarcely trustworthy. His features and gait are highly suggestive of a gorilla. Perhaps he knows something about the skis and other articles which so mysteriously disappeared from our depot.

Today the mixed-blood tells me the story of his life. Truly the poor fellow has suffered trials enough. His boat was shattered on the rock coast. The entire cargo was lost. The inland Eskimos appropriated his tent and other articles and left him to his own resources. His wife, Tom Thumb, and he spread the mainsail over oars, which they bound together as tent poles, to make an emergency shelter. For two days he lay with his wife, snowed under, in this 'tent'. In the place where he had suffered shipwreck the arctic foxes were so numerous that he could hardly frighten them off. Not content to wait until he died, they began to gnaw at his fur boots while he lay buried in the snow.

I repeat the mixed-blood's story exactly as he related it. If the reader finds it too strong, he may water it down.

OCTOBER 23

Pleasant mild weather; heavy snow last night and all of today. Laughing Boy has shot a caribou — his first on the journey. He is an egoist and usually keeps what he kills exclusively for his own use. When we others are luckY in hunting we share with everyone after the good old Eskimo custom and let the entire company taste roast meat. But Laughing Boy does not heed this practice. He has numerous family to provide for, so we indulge him; when we have made a kill he receives his share just the same.

I am now beginning to understand why Laughing Boy, despite his agreeable manners, does not enjoy the whole-hearted friendship of his fellow tribesmen. He disregards the Golden Rule that one should do to others that he would have others do to him. In general this law is better observed among Eskimos than among so-called Christians.

Towards evening the sky becomes perfectly clear and the temperature drops sharply. The northern lights are dancing wildly; they roam over the sky in a hundred shapes and colors. They change from deep green and orange-red to violet and purple. The entire sky becomes blood-red to conclude the display. The sorcerer predicts that we shall soon have a prolonged and severe snowstorm.

OCTOBER 26

After a mild day and heavy snowfall we have very bad weather again today. The temperature goes down to -23 degrees Celsius, not in itself excessively cold; but, at this season we are not yet adjusted to it. In the moist, penetrating sea air -20 degrees Celsius can be most unpleasant, especially for us with insufficient clothing. Another blizzard has blown up and confines me to my tent. Our supplies are nearly exhausted, and this evening I used my last fuel. Of the petroleum that I recently fetched up barely enough is left to boil a cup of tea. No one can conceive the value of a cup of tea in these conditions; he must feel the need in his own person.

OCTOBER 27

The blizzard is raging as if the Last Trumpet had sounded. It is impossible to leave the tent. I am completely snowed in. Even now, at midday, it is almost dark inside. Everything is frozen through and through — even the inner tent. Not a drop of petroleum left in the tent. From time to time I chop up a little ice to relieve my burning thirst.

Today I made my will, I have no hope of getting out alive if cold and blizzard last much longer. The circulation must grow sluggish in such weather when one is insufficiently clothed, without heat and crouched in a narrow tent affording no space to warm oneself by exercise.

The clothes I wear are stiff with frost. I shall crawl back into my sleeping bag, to thaw out my frozen rags a little.

After the great blizzard which plagued us from 26 to 28 October we were able to move from our tents into houses of a kind of snow and ice. The snow was not yet firm enough for the construction of regular dome-shaped snowhouses. We had recourse to large ice blocks set side by side, filled up the gaps with snow and so made the walls tight. Had we used blocks only, the wind would have whistled through the gaps. We used an old tent for a roof.

Naturally these huts of snow and ice mixed are not particularly warm. But at least we are sheltered from the biting wind. In the tent the temperature had differed little from that in the open air. In these ice-houses it was about -10 degrees Celsius, while outside the temperature ranged from -20 degrees Celsius to -30 degrees Celsius.

The mixed-blood keeps on demanding of the Eskimos whether the condition of snow and surface will not soon be good enough to permit our escaping to the south by komatik. He wishes to go back to Churchill as soon as he can with his wife. I must get back there too, to buy from the Indians summer caribou hides for new winter clothing. I have already mentioned that we lost our stock of hides in the shipwreck, and no new skins of the right kind are procurable in the Barren Lands.

Caribou are now quite numerous hereabouts and, in consequence, so are the wolves. The arctic wolf so closely resembles the Eskimo dog that I often find it difficult to tell them apart. They are similar in their ways: They form themselves into smaller or larger packs and howl most pitifully. The Eskimos say that their dogs are descended from wolves. Their forefathers were wolves, caught young, tamed and used for domestic purposes. Even today there are instances of wolves pairing with dogs. Observation shows that only the males of the two species fight with one another. Never will the male dog attack a she-wolf or the male wolf start upon a she-dog.

The arctic foxes also are plentiful. They follow wolf and caribou and live on what the wolf leaves over from his meal. When caribou are as numerous as they are just now in this region the wolves dine plentifully and there is so much left over that even the ever-hungry arctic fox has a full stomach.

The mixed-blood and I are busy making preparations for the journey. He and his spouse have no dogs; I must make room for his baggage on my komatik.

By the beginning of November the ice-cover on the rivers near our camp seems to be tolerably safe; but on land the snow has not yet attained the desired depth. We can load only the most indispensable items on our komatiks: sleeping bags, some foodstuff, ammunition, tobacco and matches.

It is most essential that we have as few people as possible riding on the komatik — an important point when we have grandmothers tagging after us. We have only six dogs for ourselves; we cannot expect too much from such a team on stony ground. The rest of the dogs are reserved for our friends who remain at the camp, so that in case of necessity they not be altogether helpless. With a vivid recollection of the voyage up here in an overloaded boat, I request that the man with the borrowed wife accompany me on the journey to the south. It is my conjecture that few of the others will wish to come along, if he accompanies me. He is reputed to be 'not quite right in the head.' But I find him by no means stupid. Only one young fellow, a relative of the half-wit, goes with us, apart from the mixed-blood and his wife. The borrowed wife remains here; she will be borrowed by another man under whose protection she will await the reappearance of her stupid husband.

After another blizzard which I weather comfortably in my house of ice and snow, the snow is at last firm enough for the building of dome-shaped snowhouses. Solemnly we celebrate our entry into the snowhouse of shining whiteness. It is much warmer than the ice-hut, and the snuggest dwelling imaginable in the Arctic. Snow is a poor conductor of heat, so that warmth and cold penetrate it very slowly. Even at -40 degrees Celsius in the open air one can raise the temperature in a new snowhouse to a few degrees above freezing, providing that there are enough people inside it and the Eskimos' oil lamps are burning. It is thus that one usually warms a newly built house. If the inner walls begin to melt, one makes an opening in the dome, whereby cold air pours in and stiffens the wall with frost.

When the air in the snowhouse is foul with the smoke of the blubber lamp, a hole appears of itself in the dome — sometimes even a number of little holes — and fresh air is admitted. If it then becomes too cold, the holes are stopped with handfuls of snow, and everything is once more as it should be. This process is remarkably simple and effective.

A piece of ice serves as a window; carefully cut and thoroughly polished until it is thin and smooth and affords a passage to the light of the sun. The window is placed over the entrance which is usually on the south or southwest side.

The ice-house, or one built of stone, unless there is a stove and sufficient fuel, is as cold as a canvas tent. There is no protection except against the wind. In a snowhouse one does very well without a stove. Proper clothing, body warmth and the heat from the customary blubber lamp are enough for warmth. One seldom tries to raise the temperature above freezing point; in general that is enough, if the snowhouse is new and its snow walls not yet turned to ice. I give the Eskimos a feast to dedicate my new snowhouse. This is at the same time a farewell banquet, for I hope in a few days to be off to the south by dogteam.

The greater part of my possessions which were saved from the wreck lie tucked away now in my snow house. There are too many candles. One or two are enough to brilliantly light the whole snowhouse. The reflected light beaming back from the pure white walls and the dome multiplies the effect of the candles and lights the whole room with a solemn splendor. Snow crystals gleam and sparkle like diamonds. So a new snowhouse resembles a castle in fairyland. The laughing little Eskimo children are the elves and the goblins. The young people I treat to oatmeal and chocolate prepared from cocoa, milk powder, sugar and water. Then comes the lineup of adults whose meal is pemmican and tea.

While the Eskimos are still eating, one of Laughing Boy's half-grown sons, who had just before been here with the children, comes back and howls at the door, 'Kakonni mai!'. That means something like, 'I am dying of hunger!' That provoked a roar of laughter among the feasting guests. When one begs a meal the customary phrase is, 'Nerrijum-avunga' — 'I would be glad to eat something.' Laughing Boy's stripling had no doubt smelled my pemmican of which he had a pleasant recollection from an earlier occasion. After the men have eaten he is permitted to feast to his heart's content. In no time the little adolescent Uttuta slips into the snowhouse and keeps Laughing Boy's son company with the delicious pemmican. Otherwise they are modest and well-behaved. A little relish pleases them and they thank me very pleasantly, each in his own way: 'Krujanamik, Krujanaputit, Krujanakonni.'

On the evening preceding our departure Donald gives a dinner to all the Eskimos in the camp. He serves cooked caribou heads and raw frozen caribou marrow. That is a very choice dainty. One cannot describe the taste to those who have never experienced it. In comparison to frozen marrow the cooked article is quite insipid.

In eating the marrow bones the Eskimos use a pointed probe, specially designed for that purpose, to push the marrow out of its natural covering, the upper and lower thigh-bones. The marrow must not be frozen too hard, for then it is hard to get out and it crumbles. It tastes best when just sufficiently frozen to give it hardness.

When we have so eaten as to be comfortably filled, the sorcerer holds a spiritualist seance in which he implores the blessing of the world on our journey. He sings, dances and beats his little magic drum. He shakes his head so wildly that his long mane flutters and vibrates behind him. Now he shrieks at the top of his voice, now he plays the ventriloquist. It sounds as if a number of men were chattering and shrieking in concert. With the cry: 'Atte, atte,' the other Eskimos urge him to ever more violent movements and wilder contortions. The sweat runs down his face, and his thick blue-black hair fairly bristles when, with frantic grimaces and gestures, he runs about the room to lay hold of some cowering guest. At times he speaks in an impressive whisper from the throat or the stomach with one or another of the company — and then he seems again to yield himself to the procession of the demons. At last he appears to have overcome the foul Tornrak, who turns his face away. With a shrill cry he puts an end to the seance.

The evil spirit has acknowledged defeat. With the help of other spirits, some friendly, some neutral, he has conquered the false, malicious Tornrak who cannot look one in the eye. We need no longer stand in fear of his devilry. The good and pure spirits have pledged themselves to take the Kabluna under their protection. The sorcerer gives himself a shake, mops his brow and assures me that I can now embark on my journey without fear.